ALSO BY BETSY BYARS

BETSY BYARS

McMUMMY

VIKING

VIKING
Published by the Penguin Group
Penguin Books USA Inc., 375 Hudson Street, New York, New York 10014, U.S.A.
Penguin Books Ltd, 27 Wrights Lane, London W8 5TZ, England
Penguin Books Australia Ltd, Ringwood, Victoria, Australia
Penguin Books Canada Ltd, 10 Alcorn Avenue, Toronto, Ontario, Canada M4V 3B2
Penguin Books (N.Z.) Ltd, 182–190 Wairau Road, Auckland 10, New Zealand

Penguin Books Ltd, Registered Offices: Harmondsworth, Middlesex, England

First published in 1993 by Viking, a division of Penguin Books USA Inc.

10 9 8 7 6 5 4 3

Library of Congress Cataloging-in-Publication Data
Byars, Betsy Cromer. McMummy / Betsy Byars.   p.   cm.
Summary: Looking after an eccentric scientist's greenhouse doesn't seem
any stranger than the other odd jobs taken by Mozie and his partner Battie—
until Mozie discovers a large, mummy-shaped pod on one of the plants.
I S B N 0 - 6 7 0 - 8 4 9 9 5 - 2
[1. Moneymaking projects—Fiction. 2. Supernatural—Fiction.
3. Single-parent family—Fiction.] I. Title.
PZ7.B9836Mc 1993 [Fic]—dc20   93-16717 CIP AC

For Anna

Contents

McMUMMY

M-Mummy Pod

 IT WAS HARD to explain the Mozie look to an adult, but Batty Batson had to try because his mom thought he was just being cruel when he laughed at his sister's piano recital.

"I couldn't help laughing, Mom. I didn't want to. I just couldn't help it."

"Some things are not funny."

"I know. I know . . ."

"You don't seem to."

"Well, I do."

"Then why did you laugh?"

He decided to tell the truth. "Mozie's look made me do it," he explained.

"What are you talking about? What look?"

"I'm not sure I can describe it."

"You had better try, young man."

"Oh, sure, if you put it like that." There was something about being called young man that always made Batty get serious.

"Well, we got to the recital, and we were going to be perfect—clap when we were supposed to and sit still when we were supposed to do that."

His mother waited.

"Well, as you know, Linda was the first one. She sat down on the piano bench, and you know how sometimes cushions make a funny noise when somebody sits on them, like *Fffffff—*"

Batty started laughing remembering it, but he wisely swallowed his laughter.

"So I didn't look at Mozie, because I did not want to laugh—"

The swallowed laughter came up and burst from him. He glanced up at his mother. He wished he hadn't done that because his mother had a look of her own—his least favorite look.

He made a super effort to get control of himself. It always got the laughter out of his system, when he was with Mozie, to fall down on the ground and throw himself around. He knew his mother wouldn't be as tolerant of that kind of behavior as Mozie was.

"So she—"

Batty had to stop again. This time he got his face under control by looking down at his shoes. Batty glanced up at his mother. He felt his face was in neutral now.

But the knot of laughter was still inside. He could feel it. He knew how volcanoes felt just before they erupted.

"After the cushion went *Ffffffff* . . ."

Once again, he couldn't continue. The pressure of the inner laughter brought tears to his eyes. His shoulders began to shake.

His mother waited. His mother had the patience of a rock. She could outwait eternity.

Finally—at last—Batty got himself under control.

"See, Mom, it's a look Mozie gets on his face when something funny happens. He gets this look on his face like he knows I'm going to laugh, and he knows *I know* he knows I'm going to laugh, and the worst thing I can possibly do is laugh. And I can't help myself, Mom. I laugh."

His mother looked at him. "So, why did you look at Mozie then? If you knew it was going to make you laugh?"

"I didn't. I didn't. But knowing the look was on his face, even if I couldn't see it, was as bad as seeing it. That's all I can tell you."

"Go to your room."

"Mom—"

"Go—to—your—room." When his mom started putting extra spaces between her words, Batty knew it was hopeless.

"I'm going." Batty began walking backward as a pledge of good faith. "But Mom, I promised Mozie I would go with him to Professor Orloff's greenhouse after supper. I always go with him. Mozie has to look after his plants, and he can't go there alone because last time he went he saw this very strange thing on one of the plants—"

"You're not going anywhere. You're staying in your room."

"Mom, I have to go. There're things growing in there, and I don't mean petunias. Mozie can't go by himself. His life genuinely may be in danger."

"Go—to—your—room."

"I have to at least call and warn him."

"I'll take care of it."

"Mom, he's got to have time to get someone to go with him. There are strange, strange plants in there. Remember that movie? What was the name? You remember, a plant that ate people? You wouldn't let me watch it?"

Silence.

"Mom, I didn't want to tell you this because I didn't want you to worry, but the thing Mozie saw—the thing that scared him—Mozie saw a kind of pod. I guess you'd call it a pod. Only it wasn't shaped like, you know, beans. It was shaped more like—well, a mummy, you know, kind of little at the top and then getting wider, like for a body.

"Mozie said it was covered with very, very fine hair like Grandma's cheeks."

Even this detail didn't impress his mother. He continued.

"Remember when he came over to the house yesterday? Did you happen to see him? He was waiting on the steps for me to get home from the dentist. Did you see him?"

No answer.

"Because he came running over to the car and he had a very strange look on his face."

Now his mother spoke. "*The* look?"

"No, Mom, of course not. This was a look I'd never seen before, and I've known Mozie since first grade. I said, 'What's wrong?' because I knew immediately something had happened. He drew me aside. He said, 'There's a m-mummy pod in the greenhouse.'

"I thought he said McMummy and I go, 'Man, you been eating too many hamburgers.' "

His mother did not look amused at his humor.

"Mozie said, 'I am telling the truth. There is a m-mummy pod on the big plant in the back. Come with me tomorrow. See for yourself.' He said, 'Promise, because I'm not going there alone.'

"I said, 'I promise.' It was an actual promise." He crossed his heart as earnestly as he used to when he was little.

"I know you are very big on keeping promises because when I promised not to eat anything chewy with my new braces and you came in and caught me eating a Snickers bar, I honestly thought you were going to hit me."

His mother looked at him, and he trailed off. For a moment he hoped she was softening. But then she said, "You will go to any lengths, won't you, make up any story, no matter how fantastic, to get out of the house."

"Mom, it's true. I didn't make it up. If I were going to make up something, I would make up something you would believe like homework or going to the library. I wouldn't make up a McMummy pod because there is no such thing."

"Exactly. Now go to your room."

"Mom, can I ask you one thing?"

She waited.

"Mozie and I are baby-sitting Friday night and I need to tell him if I can't go."

"You can't go."

"Mom, these are jobs! You want me to be a success in life, don't you? You want me to get off the dole, don't you? You—"

"I want you to go to your room. Your father will be in to talk to you when he gets home from Atlanta."

"About what?"

"Your sister's piano recital."

"Oh, that."

Now Batty went.

As the Mummy Turns

MOZIE WALKED UP the steps to Batty's house. He took a deep breath and rang the bell. Mozie hoped Batty himself would answer instead of one of his sisters—especially Linda. She would still be mad about the recital and probably wouldn't let him in.

The door opened. It was Mrs. Batson. This was better than Linda but worse than one of the other two sisters.

Mozie cleared his throat. "Could I speak to Batty? I forgot to tell him something."

"Who?"

Mrs. Batson's voice was cold. Mozie remembered that she didn't like Batty to be called Batty. Her husband, Mr. Batson, was also called Batty, so now she had the burden of living with Little Batty and Big Batty, which Mozie knew couldn't be pleasant.

To everybody else in the world they were Mozie Mozer and Batty Batson, but to Mrs. Batson, they were Robert and Howard.

Mozie corrected himself at once. "Could I speak to Robert, please?"

"No."

"Isn't he here?" Mozie tensed with alarm. "Mrs. Batson, he and I are going up to Professor Orloff's. I have a job watering his greenhouse and, for reasons I won't go into, Batty has to go with me today. When will he be back? I'll just wait for him unless he's going to be very late—he will be back before dark, won't he?"

"Robert has not gone out, Howard. He is in his room."

"Oh, good. What a relief. I'll go up."

Mrs. Batson seemed to expand so that she filled the whole doorway, making it impossible for Mozie to get in the house. Her voice—though it had been stern enough to start with—got sterner.

"Howard, I want to say something to you."

"Yes, of course, but make it—" He was about to add "snappy," but, fortunately for him, she interrupted.

"Howard, I want you to stop giving Robert looks."

Mozie was so stunned he couldn't answer for a moment. He had never actually given Batty a look, and certainly not at his sister's piano recital. Once he glanced at Batty in assembly when the Suzuki violins had gotten off to a bad start on "Mississippi Hotdog," but it wasn't a look. The fact that Batty laughed didn't make it a look.

Mrs. Batson waited a reasonable length of time for him to recover and then asked, "Did you hear me?"

"I don't give him looks. He thinks I give him looks, b-but I don't. I really don't even have a look, if you want the truth. I couldn't even give him a look if I wanted to. I mean, this *is* my look, Mrs. Batson. My face just looks like I'm giving a look, even though I don't have a look to give. I m-mean, I can't—"

The only time Mozie ever stuttered was when he was trying to explain something to Batty's mom—or when he saw a mummy pod.

Mrs. Batson interrupted. "I do not have time to listen to foolishness."

"It's not foolishness—it's the truth," he began. Then, because the situation was so desperate, he decided to beg.

"Mrs. Batson, please, please, Robert's got to go to the greenhouse with me. He's got to!"

"Robert only has to do one thing this evening, and that's stay in his room. His behavior at the recital was inexcusable."

"Mrs. Batson, I can't go out to the greenhouse by myself.

I didn't want to mention this, but yesterday when I was there—remember Batty was at the dentist?—well, yesterday, I saw this sort of pod. It was shaped like a mummy, and, um, I know you're going to think I'm being foolish, imagining things even, but the pod seemed to move, to turn in my direction like, well, radar."

He swallowed.

"I'm really, honestly scared, Mrs. Batty—I m-mean Mrs. Batson."

He closed his eyes, trying for self-control.

"I mean, once you've seen a mummy pod, and it sort of turns in your direction, you don't ever want to see it happen again. If Batty's there, he can stop me from—"

"I'm not going to listen to any more of this talk about a mummy pod. You boys have gone too far this time. Goodbye, Howard."

"Mrs. Batson, please! Just let me say one more thing."

She waited in a silence so cold it seemed to chill the air.

"Mrs. Batson, I know you are a person of honor because Ba—Robert has told me that many, many times, and you would—I am sure—always want Robert to keep his word—his promise."

He swallowed, and the sound was like a word out of a guttural foreign language.

"Now," he continued, "I think I see a way that Robert could keep his solemn word to me as well as be punished. That way, Mrs. Batson, would be for you to let him go with me this afternoon and start his punishment tomorrow—"

"The punishment has already started. Good-bye, Howard."

She closed the door.

Mozie stood for a moment without moving. Then he walked quickly to the side of the house and looked up at Batty's window.

Batty's face was there, pulled into an expression of concern. He opened the window and leaned out. "I'm grounded. You heard her."

"Batty, I'm really scared to go back to the greenhouse by myself."

"I'm scared for you."

"You're not as scared as I am."

There was a long silence as they looked at each other.

Mozie felt that the distance between him and Batty was more than one story of a house. Batty was miles away, up in an unreachable place that might as well have been the moon.

"If only you hadn't given me the look," Batty said.

"I didn't!"

Batty shook his head with real regret. "If only I hadn't thought you were giving me the look."

"Yes. Good-bye, Batty."

P! L! A! N! T! S!

MOZIE OPENED the front door and stepped into the hall. He glanced at himself in the mirror.

His expression was, as usual, pleasant. The expression was built-in. He had an elf face. Everything turned up—his nose, the corners of his mouth, his eyes.

What would it take to make his face look pitiful? he wondered. Here he was facing a pod-shaped mummy—alone! And he was powerless against this pod! And yet he looked as if he was going to pull on a pointed hat and help St. Nick.

In the living room a voice said, "I'm going to say my philosophy of life for you, if you don't mind hearing it again."

Miss Tri-County Tech was practicing her philosophy of life in the living room as Mozie's mother fitted her dress.

Mozie's mother made a living sewing beautiful dresses for pageants. She didn't make dresses for Miss South Carolina and Mrs. America. She was on a lower level of pageantry. She sewed for Miss County Fairground and Miss Goober and Junior Miss Buncombe County.

"Ouch!"

"Oh, did I stick you? Sorry."

"That's okay," Miss Tri-County Tech said. "My philosophy of life is this. Be not what you are, but what you are capable of being. Make every minute count. Spend time with yourself and your other loved ones. You will only pass this way wunst."

"Once," Mrs. Mozer corrected.

"I can never remember not to put a *t* on *once*. Once! Once! Once! You will only pass this way ONCE. I wonder why once doesn't have a *t* on the end of it. It needs one. Doesn't wunst sound better than once? It does to me."

From the hall Mozie interrupted quietly but firmly. "Mom."

"I'm in the middle of a fitting," his mother reminded him.

"I have to talk to you."

"Well, go ahead. I can listen from here."

Mozie was not allowed in the living room while his mother was having a fitting, lest he see one of the beauty contestants in a state of undress. Actually, many of the contestants were not beautiful—some were even ugly—and Mozie was happy to stay out of the way.

Still, he had many conversations with his mother like this, back to the wall, looking up. By now he was familiar with every crack, every stain in the ceiling.

"Mom, I can't go to the greenhouse because Batty's grounded."

"Well, you aren't grounded. You can still go."

"I can't. I can't go by myself. Mom, I didn't want to tell you this because I knew you would either: (1) not believe me or (2) not care."

In the living room Miss Tri-County Tech said, "Remember to make the dress real tight in the waist because I'm going to lose ten pounds by next Saturday."

"We can always take it in," his mother said sensibly, "but if I have to let it out, sometimes the stitch marks show, particularly in satin."

Mozie ground his teeth in frustration. His mother was sensible about everything but him.

"Mom?"

"Mozie, are you still there?"

"Yes, I am still here."

"Well, go on with what you were saying."

"I was saying that—well, even when I first started in the greenhouse, I had an uneasy feeling. That was why I always took Batty with me. He was uneasy too. But we didn't know why. It was just all these plants!"

"Mozie, that's what a greenhouse is for—plants. You knew there would be plants there when you agreed to do this."

"Yes, plants! Lettuces and radishes and cherry tomatoes—those kind of plants. These are P! L! A! N! T! S!"

"Don't be dramatic," his mother said.

Miss Tri-County Tech said, "If I win, I'm going to say, 'I owe my success to God and to my country and to my boyfriend Bucky Buckaloo.' "

Mozie said patiently, "Mom."

"Bucky doesn't know I'm going to put him up there with God and country. It's going to blow his mind."

"Mom." Still he was patient.

"Yes, Mozie, I'm listening. Go on about the greenhouse."

Although Mozie could not see his mom's expression, he knew exactly how her face looked when she was disinterested. It would look that way now. He continued anyway.

"Well, always the greenhouse has given me an uneasy feeling, but I didn't say anything because we needed the money."

"I appreciate that," his mother said, then to Miss Tri-County Tech, "put this tissue in your mouth so we don't get lipstick on the front of the dress."

"But yesterday when I was there, I was alone—Batty was at the dentist getting braces—I got this strange feeling . . ."

Mozie paused because the feeling came back to him as he stood in his own hallway—a strange feeling of dread and fascination.

He had been deep in the greenhouse at the back, where the largest plants grew. He had been drawn there for some reason he couldn't explain. He had never ventured back there before. Usually he came just inside the door of the greenhouse, where the controls for the sprinkler system were.

The instructions for him were posted there. The writing was in Professor Orloff's thin precise script.

1. Make sure the timer is set for exactly three hours.
2. Open valve X. Put one vial of liquid Vitagrow into valve.
3. Close valve tightly.
4. Turn on sprinkler system. Wait to see it is operational.
5. Exit and lock door.

Each time before he had done exactly as instructed. He would come just inside the door while Batty waited behind him.

"I'll wait outside," Batty would say. "One of us has to be out of reach. Remember that movie with that plant that

ate people? What was the name? It was a singing plant, but
it ate people between songs. I think of that plant every time
I come to the greenhouse."

Mozie could not explain what had drawn him forward
this time. He was afraid to venture into the greenhouse and
yet he went anyway, as if he couldn't help himself. Like a
person sleepwalking, he moved down the aisle of greenery
so overgrown that he had to bend to avoid the heavy leaves.

On either side grew tomatoes as big as basketballs. Squash
that would take two men to lift drooped on their thick
vines. Flowers like trumpets pointed at him as if to blow
an alarm. Cucumbers as big as watermelons lay on the
ground.

At the end of the greenhouse he had stopped. Here were
the biggest, strangest of the plants. The heavy limbs brushed
the top of the greenhouse. The stems were as big as Mozie's
body. The leaves were like flying carpets.

Mozie stood there, awed and afraid. His arms trembled
at his sides.

And then he had reached out with one trembling hand
and pushed the huge leaves aside. He drew in a breath. He
almost choked as the thick, rich air hit his lungs.

His heart began to race as he saw what was hidden in the
leaves.

There was a pod.

A pod as big as his own body—thick and heavy with a
faint green hair covering it. The sunlight made it shiver and

then—though it could have been a movement of the sunlight—that's what Mozie hoped it was—the pod seemed to turn toward him.

At that moment, Mozie himself had turned and run for the door. He started the hundred-yard dash toward the woods, stopped, turned, and ran back to the greenhouse.

He had left the door open and he leaned inside. With trembling hands he opened valve X, put in the Vitagrow, turned on the sprinkler system, closed the door, locked it.

This time, running for home, he didn't stop for anything.

A Girl Named
Valvoline

 "MOZIE, are you still out there in the hall?"

His mother's voice drew Mozie abruptly back to the present.

"Yes, I am still here."

"Are you finished with what you were saying?"

In the hall, Mozie's heart was racing as it had yesterday.

"Mom, I'm not kidding about this. I really am afraid of going to the greenhouse. Because yesterday, I didn't want to walk back there to that plant. I did not want to! And I did. That's what really scares me. I was actually drawn against my will—I know you think I'm being dramatic, but . . ."

In the living room his mother said, "Now, Valvoline, let's see if we can slip this over your head without sticking you again."

"I wish my name wasn't Valvoline," Miss Tri-County Tech said. "That's one reason I think I might not get it. You know what my mother told me? Ouch!"

"Sorry."

"My mother told me she had named me for somebody in a romantic novel she read, which I believed. I was so proud of my name. I wouldn't let anybody shorten it to Val. Then, then! I come to find out she got mixed up and named me for a motor oil."

"Mom."

"Yes, Mozie, I'm still listening." Her tone implied she was still listening but she was more interested even in motor oil than plants.

"I cannot go back there by myself," Mozie said in a reasonable, adultlike voice. "I need someone to make sure I do not go back to that plant!"

"Come in the living room, Mozie," his mother said. "It's safe."

Mozie peered around the door of the living room. Valvoline was dressed. She was at the mirror, fluffing her hair.

Mozie's face, he knew, would not reflect his concern. He actually feared for his life, and this little merry face . . .

He hated his face. He wanted to take his hands and re-model his face like clay, to force his features to reflect the panic that surged through his body.

"Don't pay any attention to my face," he began, "be-cause—"

"Are you talking about that old greenhouse out on Sump-ter Road?" Miss Tri-County Tech asked, turning toward him.

Mozie nodded.

"We used to go out there when we were in junior high. It was spooky back then. The big house had burned down and the plants in the greenhouse were all dried up and rattled like skeletons when the wind came in the door."

She gave her hair an additional fluff. "Maybe it's changed, but I would not let a little boy of mine go out there by himself."

Mozie said, "See, Mom, everybody knows it's dangerous but you!"

"Mozie, that was years ago. The greenhouse had been abandoned then. Now Professor Orloff's taken it over. Everyone says that eventually his discoveries will save the world. That's what he's doing at the World Congress on Hunger right now. This man may single-handedly solve the problem of world hunger."

"That doesn't help me now," Mozie said. He felt childish and selfish, standing in the way of the hungry, but he really was afraid.

His mother put Valvoline's dress on a hanger. "All right, if you don't want to go alone, get one of your friends to go with you—pay them if you have to."

"Mom, Batty's the only friend I've got."

His mother sighed now, showing her irritation. "I guess I could go. But I'll never get this gown finished by Friday."

Miss Tri-County Tech said, "Look, I could drive him out there."

His mother's face brightened. "You wouldn't mind, Valvoline?"

"I'll drive him, only I'm not going into that greenhouse. I'll park by the old Esso station and wait for him. And I'm keeping all the doors locked."

Mozie broke into the conversation. "And if I don't come back, will you call my mom?"

"I will. I'll even call 911 if it'll make you feel any better."

"Is that agreeable, Mozie?"

"Yes. But Mom, you will listen for the phone?" Sometimes his mom forgot everyday life when she sewed.

"Yes."

"Do I have time to call Batty?" Mozie asked Val. "I just want to let him know I've got help."

"Yes, but hurry, Mozie, because I have to pick Bucky up at seven."

Mozie ran upstairs and dialed Batty's number. If Mrs. Batson answered, he would, of course, hang up immediately, but he wanted his friend to know he was not going to be devoured.

The phone was picked up by one of Batty's sisters. Batty had three sisters, and they all sounded alike. Mozie hoped this one wasn't Linda, whose piano recital they had attended with such disastrous results.

"May I speak to Batty, please?"

"He can't come out of his room."

"Well, could you give him a message for me?"

"Maybe."

"Tell him that Mozie called—"

"Mozie?" She gave the name a distasteful ring. Though none of Batty's sisters liked him, Linda hated him, and he thought with a sinking heart that this was Linda.

"Yes."

"You want me to give a message to Batty?"

"Yes."

"Moi? The sister whose piano recital you completely ruined?"

Mozie hated it when Batty's sisters did their Miss Piggy routines.

"Linda"—he swallowed, making a sort of guttural sound—"I'm sorry about what happened."

"You're sorry all right."

"Please just tell him that I'm going to the greenhouse, but a girl named Valvoline's going with me and she's going to wait out by the Esso station, and if I don't come out, she's going to call my mom. I just wanted him to know because he was worried for my life and . . . Hello? Hello?"

"I'm leaving now," Valvoline called from below.

Mozie ran down the stairs.

The Quack-Quacks

 "DID YOU HAPPEN to hear my philosophy of life when I was saying it in your living room?" Valvoline asked as she made a left turn, using both lanes to complete it.

"Yes, I did."

"How did it sound?"

"Good."

"It's the same philosophy of life I used in the Miss Dogwood pageant, so I hope no one will remember."

"They won't."

"But my 'I owe my success to God and to my country' they can't remember because I didn't get to say it. One good thing about not winning that pageant was I was going with Howard Eck then, and I would have had to say, 'I owe my success to God and to my country and to my boyfriend Howard Eck.' That was one reason I broke up with him. I didn't want to be Mrs. Eck."

Valvoline and Mozie were halfway to the greenhouse when she reached out and began to fumble with the dashboard of the car.

"Is anything the matter?" Mozie asked, tightening his seatbelt.

"I'm trying to find the headlights," she explained. She pulled out the cigarette lighter. "Well, that's not them."

"No."

"Everybody else has their lights on so there's probably a storm somewhere even if we can't see it. Wonder where the headlights are."

Mozie pointed to a knob and she pulled it.

"Oh, thanks."

She pushed it back in. "Now I'm ready in case it does storm. I hope it doesn't rain for the pageant."

"Me too," Mozie said, just to be pleasant. All he cared about was getting into the greenhouse, turning on the sprinkler system, and getting back out without taking that long, unwilling, dreamlike walk to the end of the greenhouse.

"I wonder where the windshield wipers are. This isn't

my car, in case you're wondering. It's Bucky's. I'm just driving it."

Mozie pointed. "There."

"Thanks."

She flicked them on and off.

Mozie wiped his hands on the side of his pants. His palms were getting sweaty.

"Now, what's this thing you were talking about in the greenhouse?" Valvoline asked.

"A m-mummy pod."

"McMummy?"

"No, just mummy."

"I've never even heard of such a thing."

"Me either."

"What won't they think of next?"

Mozie's tension was growing. It was hard to keep up a normal conversation.

He dreaded the moment when he unlocked the greenhouse door, pushed it open, and heard that faint creak of the door's hinge—like something out of a horror movie. The memory of that creak caused him to shudder.

"You all right?"

"Yes."

"You aren't cold, are you? I could turn down the air-conditioning if I knew where it was."

"I'm fine. It's nice of you to do this."

"I don't mind. I like to drive."

"Usually I just take the shortcut through the woods."

"I hate the woods. I have been scared of woods since kindergarten when Miss Penny—she loved fairy tales—and she gave a lot of feeling to the words when she read. I can still hear her saying, 'The deep, dark woods.' I was third runner-up for Miss Dogwood last year and I believe the reason I didn't get it was because it came across that I just can't stand trees."

Mozie nodded sympathetically.

"Oh, here's the road. I was about to pass it. It's so overgrown it doesn't even look like a road."

She turned the car into the boarded-up Esso station, pulled on the hand brake, and the car skidded to a stop beside the rusty gas pumps. The two of them fell silent.

Mozie was holding his cap against his chest as if for protection. He and Batty had gotten these hats free at the opening of Ace Hardware. They were white with yellow bills, and when Batty's sister first saw them, she said, "Well, if it isn't the Quack-Quacks."

He looked out the car window at the deserted gas station. Beyond, the overgrown road was like a secret lane to nowhere.

The pause continued until Mozie said, "I guess I better get out."

"I'll be right here. I'm going to keep the engine running, and when you get through, we'll scratch off."

"Right."

"How long you think it's going to take you?"

"Ten minutes to get to the greenhouse, one minute to turn on the sprinkler, and thirty seconds to get back."

Valvoline looked blank for a minute and then smiled. "I get it. You're going to be running back."

"Yes," Mozie said emphatically.

"Let's see. How many minutes was that?"

"Eleven and a half."

"I'll give you fifteen."

Mozie nodded. "But don't leave!" he added, turning to her.

"I won't. There's a pay phone right over there, and first thing, I'll call your mom. I want to ask her something about my dress anyway. I think it needs more sequins."

Mozie didn't want to get out of the car. He knew how their dog Flexie used to feel when they arrived at the vet's. Flexie would jump in the backseat. They'd open the back door and she'd jump in the front seat. As a last resort, she would crouch down on the floor and tremble.

Valvoline reached over and opened the door for him. There was nothing to do now but get out.

He put on his cap. Remembering Batty's sister's rude remark about the caps, he turned the bill to the back. He wished earnestly that the other Quack-Quack was at his side.

"Here I go," he said.

He got out of the car and started across the hot tarmac toward the old road.

The air was still and heavy. Nothing seemed to be moving in the entire universe except his slow feet. He might as well have had on fins, he thought, he was walking so awkwardly.

He glanced back over his shoulder. Valvoline was locking all the doors of the car.

He faced forward. Manfully, but slowly, Mozie headed up the road. The sign ahead read DEAD END.

The Sound of Thunder

MOZIE PAUSED outside the greenhouse.

It was a huge old building constructed twenty years ago by the town's only millionaire, Mr. Downs. Hobart Downs had had a love of exotic tropical plants, and he raised them in the greenhouse and brought them up to the big house on trucks.

After Mr. Downs's death, the mansion and the greenhouse fell into disuse. The house burned to the ground during an electrical storm, and the greenhouse and gardener's cottage had been bought two years ago by Professor Orloff.

Mozie pushed open the door. The faint creak of the hinges brought goose bumps to his arms. He wished for Batty. He knew Valvoline was waiting at the old Esso station, but that wasn't like having Batty right behind him. He longed to hear Batty say, "I'm right behind you, pal, and I won't push."

Mozie took a deep, purposeful breath because he didn't want to risk having that heady, peculiar air of the greenhouse in his lungs. He took one step inside the greenhouse, one more step to the sprinkler system.

His hand reached for valve X. He turned the valve and reached for a bottle of Vitagrow—a strange-looking liquid, brownish in color with a distasteful smell. Mozie poured the foul liquid into the valve and closed it.

Mozie was still holding his breath though his face was turning red. He was reaching for the sprinkler system when suddenly, he paused.

He stood for a moment without moving. Then, slowly, he let out his breath and inhaled the thick, scented air of the greenhouse. He turned and faced the rear where THE plant grew.

Everything seemed to have grown since he was here yesterday. The plants' limbs reached out over the aisle, forming a sort of arch that led him forward. Some of the trumpetlike flowers had fallen to the ground, and in their place vegetables were already beginning to form.

Slowly Mozie began to move down the aisle, the arch of branches closing over his head. Huge leaves brushed his cheeks. He stepped over a squash that had fallen and now blocked his way.

He felt as if he had shrunk, like in a science-fiction movie, where normal blades of grass were like skyscrapers.

To ease his fears, he began a conversation with the absent Batty, taking both sides himself.

"Well, Batty, I'm inside. You wait outside, like you always do, all right?"

"Okey-doke!"

"Make sure I come out?"

"Okey-doke."

"If I don't, get the police. They'll know what to do."

"Okey-doke."

The "okey-dokes," spoken in what really sounded to him like Batty's voice, helped lift Mozie's spirits. He went deeper into the greenhouse. He could not explain why he continued. He didn't want to go in. He wanted to be running for the Esso station and Valvoline's car.

He paused at the end of the greenhouse where he had stopped yesterday. This time he did not reach out and push the leaves aside. He knew what was behind them.

"I'm not going to look, Batty," he said.

"Okey-doke," he answered for Batty.

And yet even as he spoke his hand reached toward the leaves. Carefully, trying to disturb as little as possible, Mozie shifted the leaves aside.

There was the pod.

It was bigger than it had been yesterday, so heavy now that it seemed impossible the stem could hold it. The bottom of the pod rested on the rich black soil.

"It's either the dirt or that stinking Vitagrow stuff," Batty had said yesterday when Mozie told him about the mummy pod. "Remember? I never did trust that dirt."

"The dirt?"

"Yeah, that dirt. Remember? That's one reason I didn't want to go in there because I didn't like the smell of that dirt. It's like one million B.C. dirt. Smelling it could be bad for you. It could cause something." Batty was afraid of inhaling anything that didn't smell right.

"I don't think there's anything wrong with the dirt," Mozie had said.

To add credit to his theory, Batty had said, "I bet it came from Egypt."

"Egypt?"

"Well, it would explain the mummy pod," Batty had answered defensively. "If it is a mummy pod, you know what's got to be in it, don't you? A mummy! And you know what mummies do to you, don't you?"

Mozie said, "What?" He knew what werewolves did to

you, and vampires, but he wasn't sure about mummies.

"They—they put an ancient curse on you. That's what they do!"

The soil did give off a scent richer, more exotic, than local fields. It did smell, Mozie thought now, as he stood deep in the greenhouse, sort of like the Nile. Mozie had never been to the Nile, but he had seen pictures of it, and this was the way it looked like it would smell.

Mozie didn't know where it came from, but he was sure he would never, ever forget the smell of the greenhouse. For the rest of his life—assuming he got out of here—whenever he saw a picture of the Nile, this rich, exotic scent would fill his nostrils.

Mozie shifted, but the pod did not move. Perhaps, Mozie thought, it did lean a little forward toward him, straining on its stem, but it didn't turn.

He suddenly felt that there was something inside the pod—an actual presence, a being. It scared him, and yet there was a strange feeling he had not felt before—a feeling he could not put a name to. It wasn't kinship, of course, it wasn't compassion, but it was something like those feelings. Mutual loneliness, perhaps.

He caught his breath. He and the pod were mutually alone. He sat down.

"If you're in there," Mozie said, speaking in a low voice, "I'm just, you know, a kid that's turning on the sprinkler system. Professor Orloff will be back soon. He's supposed to already be back, though he paid me until next Saturday.

"The professor's the one who can help you. You just need to hang in there until next week.

"I sort of know how you feel because my dad's gone, and when someone goes out of your life—someone you really need—well, it does make you lonely. But the professor will be coming back, and my dad won't. That's the difference, so you don't—"

There was the distant sound of thunder, and Mozie lifted his head and looked up through the dusty panes of glass overhead.

A broad line of thunderstorms had been stalled over the mountains for days, never coming closer, just gaining strength. Every afternoon the tops of the cumulonimbus clouds ballooned, and lightning could be seen in the rounded domes.

At the sound of thunder, the pod seemed to quiver. It was such a quick movement—over almost as soon as it began—that Mozie wasn't sure it had happened.

"It's just thunder," he said.

He looked up at the pod. The pod almost seemed to float above the rich soil, though the end of the pod was now pressed into the earth. It was like a prehistoric plant rising from mist, a low silhouette, green and ominous in its strangeness.

Yet, there was a grace about the pod, a beauty that held

Mozie in place, that kept him here, breathing this rich, perhaps unhealthy air until—

A sound broke into Mozie's world.

Honk! HONK! HonkHonkHonk!

"Valvoline," he said. He lifted his head. "Valvoline!"

And as if a spell had been broken, he got up and ran for the door.

911

 VALVOLINE LEANED OUT of the phone booth as Mozie ran around the corner of the gas station.

"I was worried about you, Mozie. I was calling for help. I already dialed the nine."

"I—I—"

He was too winded to speak.

Valvoline hung up the phone and stepped outside of the booth.

"What happened? I waited and waited, and ten minutes

went by, and twenty, and finally I said, 'Well, I have to call Mrs. Mozer,' and I got in the phone booth and guess what? Somebody had torn the Mozer page right out of the phone book, and I don't know your number. So then I just said, 'Well, shoot, I'm calling 911,' and I put in a dime and dialed a nine when you came running out of nowhere. You all right?"

"Yes."

"That pod didn't try to get you or anything?"

"No."

"Because I remember a little plant I got for my seventh birthday and it opened and caught flies. You could see the fly's little legs sticking out for the longest time."

"This isn't that kind of pod."

"What kind is it?"

"For one thing, it's shut."

"That doesn't mean it couldn't open."

"True."

They started for the car. "Anyway, I'm glad I didn't finish the 911 with you being all right. This friend of mine dialed 911 because her cat got his paws stuck in the VCR. And she called 911 and she didn't say it was a cat. She just said, 'It's stuck in the VCR. I can't get it out of the VCR!' And when they came and saw Bosco—"

Mozie stopped abruptly.

"What's wrong, Mozie?"

"I forgot to turn on the sprinklers."

"You mean you got to go back?"

"Yes."

"Well, I'm not going to sit out here in this deserted parking lot by myself. That's dangerous too. All kinds of cars rode by with people looking funny at me. Get in the car. I'll drive up there."

"You're sure?"

She threw the car in gear and backed out of the station. Slowly she began the drive through the thick trees.

"This is just the way I remember it from junior high," she said. "My boyfriend's mother raised Dobermans and the back of her station wagon was a sort of pen, and some people always had to ride in the pen and they hated it because they always got out smelling like Doberman . . ."

She trailed off as she came to the greenhouse. She pulled on the hand brake, and the car skidded to a stop on the gravel.

"I'm not staying in this car by myself either."

They got out together and proceeded to the greenhouse. In his haste, Mozie hadn't locked the door and he pushed it open.

"The sprinkler system is right here. It won't take but a minute."

Valvoline was beside him. She was even better than Batty as security because she gave off a sort of perfumed warmth, while Batty's warmth gave off the scent of wet sneakers.

"Wait. Don't turn it on yet."

Mozie froze with his hand halfway to the valve.

"I want to see it."

"The pod?"

"Yes."

She shuddered and grinned. "I love stuff like that. I guess it's being in the greenhouse where I used to come and do crazy stuff in junior high, but I want to see this pod."

"If you're sure . . ."

"Where is it?"

"Back there."

"Hold on to me," Valvoline urged.

Mozie took her arm. As they started down the aisle, walking slowly toward the plant, Mozie knew how it would feel to be walking down the aisle of the church one day, fearful of and yet hopeful for the future. He hoped the bride at his side smelled like Valvoline.

"This is it?"

"Yes."

"But I don't see any pod."

"Back there."

Mozie pulled aside the leaves and Valvoline peered in. "Well, I'll be," she said. "You know what that reminds me of?"

"A mummy."

"How'd you know I was going to say that?" She turned to grin over her shoulder at Mozie. "Is there anything inside?"

"I'm pretty sure there is."

Valvoline pulled aside some lower leaves and searched the ground. "I was hoping we'd find one lying on the ground, you know—a little one, and we could cut it open."

"I think there's just the one."

Valvoline's eyes shone as she spun around. Her hair flew out, brushing Mozie's face.

"I want to listen to it."

"What?"

"I want to get in there and listen, see if I hear anything."

"I don't think you should. We're not even supposed to be back here, Valvoline. If Professor Orloff should come walking in—and he's overdue now—well, he—"

"Oh, that old man. I saw him on the noon news one time talking about his wegetables—he can't even pronounce a *v*. He'd probably say my name was Walwoline."

She turned to the plant and wiggled her shoulders purposefully.

"I'm going in. Hold on to me," she told Mozie. "And don't let go no matter what!"

The Purr of a Tiger

"I DON'T THINK you should," Mozie said as he took her arm.

Ignoring him, she stepped onto the raised earth where the pod grew. Her high wedge heels dug into the soft earth, leaving deep marks.

Mozie made a mental note to smooth those marks over. If Professor Orloff saw them . . .

Valvoline was now framed in the thick leaves. She took a deep, shuddering breath. "What does it smell like in here? I've smelled this before. Now, wait, don't tell me."

She closed her eyes and inhaled again. "This is going to worry me for the rest of my life. Maybe it was that Elizabeth Taylor perfume a girl sprayed on me in Belks."

"Do you hear anything?" Mozie asked.

"Well, give me a chance."

She stepped closer to the pod. One of her shoes sunk so deeply into the earth that she lost her footing. She fell forward and clutched the pod for support.

"Valvoline!" Mozie cried in alarm.

"I'm all right. I didn't mean to hug it around the neck though." She remained for a moment with both arms draped around the pod before she straightened.

Mozie put his free hand over his heart. He leaned forward to look up at the stem. It was unbroken.

"Be careful, Valvoline. This is a valuable plant. And I'm responsible for it."

"I'm not going to hurt your old plant."

Valvoline put her ear against the pod. "I've got real good hearing. I'm like one of those things doctors use to . . ." She trailed off. There was a moment of silence.

"Do you hear anything?"

"Hush. I'm listening."

There was another long pause. Then Valvoline said, "I think I do hear something. It's *hmmmmmmmmmmm*, like that— like a bee, far, far away. Come on inside and listen."

"I—I—"

"Oh, come on. It's not going to eat you."

She reached out, and with one swift move—it was like the crack of a whip—Valvoline pulled Mozie through the foliage and into the bower where the pod rested.

He looked down—his sneakers were leaving prints too—more marks to erase. Then he looked up.

There was the pod. He could see every detail now—the faint green fuzz that covered the shiny surface, the seam down the side where it would eventually open, the heavy brown stem that held it in place, the leaves as large as pillow cases.

He could smell a heady scent too—maybe it was the pod, maybe Valvoline. It all made him think he was going to faint.

"Put your ear over here beside mine. I figure this would be where his heart is—if he's got one."

Mozie took a step forward and laid his cheek against the pod. His own heart was pounding so loudly he couldn't hear anything, even if there was something to hear.

"You hear the *hmmmmmm!*"

He swallowed. "Not yet."

He closed his eyes. He concentrated on the pod . . . on what was inside the pod. He was like a doctor concentrating on what was inside a patient. And then he did hear something—a humming sound.

"Do you hear it?"

"Yes. I hear something, but it doesn't sound like a bee."

"It did to me." She listened again. "But now it's getting louder, don't you think?"

"Maybe."

"You know what it reminds me of?"

Mozie turned his head so that they faced each other. He looked into her wide eyes. "What?"

"I was getting ready to say, it reminded me of a cat purring."

"Yes."

"Only now, for some reason, I'm beginning to think it sounds like a bigger animal. It's the purr of a tiger."

"Well, I've never heard a tiger."

"You don't have to hear one to know what one sounds like!"

Valvoline grinned. "Knock knock." She rapped on the pod.

"Valvoline," Mozie creid. He was as upset as if she'd rapped on a valuable mummy in a museum.

"I just want to see if it's hollow." Her face lit up. "Let's plug it."

"What's that?" he asked, even though it didn't sound like anything he wanted to be a part of.

"If you're in a watermelon patch, and you don't want to go to the trouble of carrying a bad watermelon all the way to the car, well, you cut a little plug about that big and—"

Now he was truly horrified. "Get out of here right now, Valvoline. I mean it. I'm in charge and—"

She didn't move. Instead she lifted her head as if with sudden thought.

"You know what? My friend used to have this bald-headed Buddha doll, and she'd rub its head three times and make a wish. That's how she got to be a cheerleader, because she sure couldn't cheer." She looked up at the pod. "I just have this feeling . . ."

She put her hand on the top of the pod and rubbed it three times. "Please let me be Miss Tri-County Tech. Please let me be Miss Tri-County Tech. Please let me be Miss Tri-County Tech."

Thunder rumbled in the distance, and there was a faint trembling motion of the pod.

"Did you feel that?" Valvoline asked.

"Yes. There was thunder a little while ago and it did the same thing."

Valvoline put her head against the pod and listened. "It's stopped going *hmmmmmm*."

Mozie listened too. The pod was silent.

Valvoline hugged the mummy. "Don't you worry," she said, "I'm not going to let anything get you."

Crumb Castle #3

 VALVOLINE PULLED on the hand brake and the car skidded to a stop, leaving black tire marks on the Mozers' driveway.

"I'm going in with you," she said. "Wishing on a pod is one thing, but it's not going to hurt my odds to have some sequins on the back of my dress."

She turned off the engine, got out of the car, and turned back to Mozie.

"Aren't you coming?"

"In a minute." He opened his door.

Mozie got out of the car slowly. He could still hear the hum within the pod. It stuck in his brain. It left him with a strange feverish feeling. He almost felt as if he were under a spell.

He started up the walk. Valvoline was already up the steps and inside by the time he got to the porch. Mozie sat down.

Mozie and his mom lived in a house that his mom called Crumb Castle #3. There had been two other Crumb Castles in two other cities, but Mozie couldn't remember them. He had seen pictures of them, however, and they lived up to their names—the crumb part anyway.

It was seven o'clock in the evening, but the sun was still hot, and the windows of the house were open. Crumb Castle wasn't air-conditioned. Mozie could hear the sound of his mother's sewing machine and then Valvoline's interruption.

"Mrs. Mozer, I'm back."

"Oh? Is Mozie—"

"He's fine. He's on his way in." Valvoline paused. "Mrs. Mozer, I love my dress—you know that—but I've started worrying about its not having sequins on the back."

"You wanted to keep the cost down."

"Yes, but I want to win more than I want to keep the cost down."

Mozie's cat, Pine Cone, came out of the bushes, and Mozie coaxed him over.

"Come on, Pine Cone, come here, boy," he said. Pine Cone ignored him and licked his back paw.

No one believed Mozie, but Pine Cone had fallen out of an airplane and landed in the yard. Crumb Castle was at the end of runway 28 of the local airport, and one day a plane was taking off and Mozie heard something crashing through the pine tree in the yard. He ran over, and Pine Cone was holding on to the last limb. His eyes were wild— as anybody's would be who had just fallen from an airplane.

Pine Cone hung for a moment and then dropped and lay in a crouch. Mozie ran in the house. "Mom, a cat fell out of a plane!"

"Oh, Mozie."

"It did. It's lying under the pine tree. I don't think it can move."

"No cat could survive falling from a plane."

"Even people survive sometimes. I'm calling the airport."

He called the airport and said, "This is not a crank call, but are you missing a cat? I think one fell out of an airplane."

"Big brown cat?"

"Yes."

"That's him. Is he dead?"

"No, but he's not moving around." Mozie checked out the window and the cat was still in a crouch, looking more like a fallen pine cone than a cat.

"He's just a stray—got in the bad habit of crawling up in airplanes. I guess he thought he was still on the ground and decided to get out."

"Are you going to come for him?"

"He'll come back if he wants to."

So far Pine Cone had not wanted to have anything more to do with the airport. Mozie really liked Pine Cone, and when he came up and let Mozie scratch his neck, Mozie felt as proud as if it were the President of the United States who'd offered his neck to be scratched.

"Come here, Pine Cone, come here, boy."

Pine Cone looked at Mozie as if he were trying to figure out who he was.

"Come on, it's me, Moze."

He scratched his nails against the steps, and Pine Cone came over.

"Good Pine Cone!" he said. He began to scratch the cat behind the ears. "You know, Pine, to this day nobody believes that you fell out of an airplane. And nobody except Batty and Valvoline believe me about the pod. And I don't go around lying—that's what I can't understand. There is a pod. I listened to it."

Mozie put his hand on Pine Cone's side and felt the purring deep inside.

"I heard something in the pod too. I can still hear it in my head. And it reminds me of what's going on inside you right now. Valvoline was the first one to hear it and she said it was like the purr of a tiger, but . . ."

Pine Cone, suddenly tired of the conversation, turned and strolled into the bushes.

Inside Valvoline said, "I have to turn around. It's in the

rules. See, I walk out like this . . . I turn . . . I stay like this
till I count to ten—and ten is long enough for the judges
to start wondering why I don't have any sequins on my
back."

"I could make a very small rose on the shoulder
strap . . . here."

"Great! Only don't make it too small, hear?"

Mozie got up slowly and went into Crumb Castle #3.

Batty

 THE PHONE RANG. Mozie picked it up and a voice said, "What happened?"

"Is this you, Batty?"

"Yes, it's the Bat. What happened at the greenhouse?"

"I thought you were grounded, that you couldn't use the phone."

"I am, only my mom and dad and sisters went to the mall. My mom said, 'You are not to touch the telephone, do you understand me?' So I put socks over my hands and I am not touching the phone.

"The only thing that worries me is that I used dirty socks—I just took them off my feet and put them on my hands. And, Moze, my mom has a nose for socks. Like I'll be at the table and I'll slip my feet out of my shoes and my mom says, 'I smell socks.' So when she gets home, I'm hoping nobody will call, because if they do, she'll say, 'I smell socks on the telephone.' Then she'll—"

"Batty."

"What?"

"I know you did not call me to talk about socks."

"No, well, I want to know what happened, but first you need to know that I don't think I'm going to be able to baby-sit with you Friday night."

"Batty!"

"Don't get on my case yet. I've got a plan that might work. I'm going to pick a time when my mom is on the phone and I walk by and say, 'I'm off to baby-sit!' And before she can react, I will be off."

"Batty, we were supposed to be in this baby-sitting fifty-fifty. I'm doing all the work."

Batty and he had had sheets of paper printed and put up around the neighborhood.

Batty Batson and Mozie Mozer
THE MACHO BABY-SITTERS CLUB
Let us take care of your cares.

Batty said, "Well, you'll get to keep all the cash this time. So, what happened at the greenhouse? Talk fast because my family might come home."

"You wasted fifteen minutes on your dirty socks."

"So we can't waste any more, right? Talk!"

"Well, did your sister tell you that Valvoline went with me?"

"Of course not. Who's Valvoline? Isn't that something for cars?"

"She's a girl that my mom's designing a dress for. And it was very strange, Batty."

"I know it's strange. We're talking mummy pod. It don't get any stranger than that."

"First I went in by myself, and I was sort of drawn forward—I didn't want to go. I had to!"

"Did Valvo-whatever-her-name-is go too?"

"No, she was in the car, but the second time—"

"You did this twice?"

"Yes, and the second time, we got right in there and listened!"

"To what?"

"The pod."

"Let me get this straight. You and this girl got in there with Big Mac?"

"Yes."

"And listened?"

"Yes."

"You put your heads on this thing?"

"Yes, Batty, we heard something. I'd never heard it hum before, but when Valvoline got in there with it, it hummed. Batty, there's something in that pod."

"What kind of something?"

"I don't know—a being."

"A bean? You think it's a bean? If that thing pops open and a bean walks out . . ."

"No, a being—*b-e-i-n-g*."

"Oh, being."

"And then the sound of thunder came—you know, from that line of thunderstorms over the mountain. It was far away, but the humming in the pod stopped and it sort of quivered."

"Quivered? How—" Batty interrupted himself, "Moze!"

"What?"

"Remember that movie we saw on the late show—*Frankenstein*? Remember how that giant bolt of lightning brought the monster to life? Remember?"

"Yes."

"Well, maybe, just maybe, the same thing's getting ready to happen here. There will be a clap of thunder that leaves everybody deaf and lightning that leaves everybody blind. WHAMMO!"

Batty made the sound of a lightning strike so convincing

that when it was over, there was a silence that made Mozie think the phone had gone dead.

"Are you still there, Batty?" he asked.

He heard Batty say, "Oh, hi, Mom, Dad. I didn't hear you come in . . . These? These are socks. You told me not to touch the phone and I wanted to obey and so the phone rang and very quickly I slipped off my socks, put them on my hands, and answered."

There was a pause. Then, "I thought it might be one of Dad's customers. I'll hang up right away."

Into the phone he said, "I'm sorry, sir, but you have reached a wrong number. Good-bye."

"So long, Batty," Mozie said.

"Your father wants to talk to you," Batty's mother said.

"About what?"

"The recital."

"Oh, sure."

Batty hung up the phone, and he and Big Batty went into Batty's room.

Mozie went to his room alone.

Professor Orloff

"NO! NO!" Mozie cried.

The pod was opening and he had to keep it shut. He had to. There was something terrible and green inside.

Mozie could not see exactly what it was—his struggles were too desperate—but he understood that his life depended upon keeping this monster inside the pod.

The color of this monstrosity was a sick, unearthly, slimy

green, and it kept oozing through the crack in the pod, trying to get out. Mozie had to get it back inside—he had to, but slime kept running down his arms and he—

"No! No!"

"Wake up, Mozie."

He felt his mother shake him and he opened his eyes. The dream had been so real that he was stunned to find he was in his bedroom. He held up his arms and marveled that they were slimeless.

"Get up."

"Why? It's night."

"Telephone."

"I'm not here," he said truthfully.

"It's Professor Orloff."

"Who?"

"Professor Orloff. Get up. It's the overseas operator. He's calling from the Congress on World Hunger."

Mrs. Mozer went back into her bedroom across the hall. Mozie heard her say, "He's on the way, Operator."

Mozie put his feet on the floor and stood up. In his brain the pod was still opening, the slime still oozing. A humming sound droned in his ears.

He crossed the hall so unsteadily he was reminded of the way Pinocchio walked before he became a real boy. His mother was waiting with the phone in her hand. Silently, she urged him to take it.

He took the phone, and his mother backed away to the dresser, giving him some privacy. She continued to watch him.

His mother was wrapped in a worn bathrobe that made her look old, and the concern on her face heightened the illusion. Mozie saw his own face in the dresser mirror behind her, and even in this moment of confusion and alarm, he looked cheerful.

"Is this Howard Mozer?" the operator asked. She spoke with such an accent that Mozie barely recognized his own name.

"Yes. I think so."

"Your party is on the line," the operator said. "Go ahead, sir."

"Allo, allo. Is dis Hovard?"

"Yes, it's me. Are you on your way home?"

"No, I'm delayed. My presentation iss delayed. You understand? Und I must make de presentation. Did you get my vire?"

"No, no, what's a vire?"

"A vire! A telegram!"

"Oh, a telegram."

His mother put one hand to her face in alarm. Then she left the room.

"De telegram telling you to discontinue de Witagrow."

"No, no, I didn't. I've been giving the Witagrow."

"Den stop."

"I will, but when will you be getting home?"

"I'll haff to call you about that later. Iss ewerything all rrright?"

"Well, there's this pod—"

"Vat? Vat? Dis connection iss bad. A pot?"

"No, pod, POD!"

"Oh, de pod, de being pod. De pod iss big, ya?"

"Yes, I saw it by accident. I know I wasn't supposed to go back there, but, anyway, did you just call it the being pod?"

His mother returned with a telegram in one hand. She held it up, asking forgiveness with her expression.

"How big?"

"It's as big as I am, and it hummed for Val—" he broke off.

"Vat? Vat? I don't hear you so goot."

"The pod hummed!" Mozie screamed in the phone.

"Dat pod is my own special inwention. It has more protein dan a cow. Outside, it is like a bean. Inside, iss a . . ."

"A what? I didn't hear you."

"A wegetable, a wegetable such as the vorld hass never seen before, a wegetable that—"

"Your three minutes are up," the operator said.

"Goot-bye, Hovard. Be a goot boy and follow instructions."

And he was gone.

"I forgot about this," his mother said, coming forward with the yellow telegram. She held it out with both hands like an offering. "It came right in the middle of Beth Ann Garner's fitting and I put it on the table and immediately covered it with a piece of cloth. I hope it wasn't important."

Mozie opened the telegram.

PRESENTATION POSTPONED STOP RETURN
DELAYED STOP DISCONTINUE FEEDING STOP
KEEP WATERING STOP WILL TELEPHONE STOP
PROFESSOR OTTO ORLOFF

"Was it really important?" his mother asked.

"I'm not sure."

"I just feel terrible that I forgot it."

Mozie started for his room. The sound of distant thunder made him pause in the doorway.

"I better go downstairs and close the windows," his mother said. "That storm has been threatening for three days now. As soon as I leave those windows open, it'll rain on the pageant dresses."

Mozie went in his room and lay down. He heard the sound of windows being closed below him—hard, BAM, BAM— as if his mother was punishing the windows because she forgot the telegram.

Then he heard again the rumble of distant thunder. His

mind turned to the greenhouse, where the pod would be hearing the same sound and trembling.

As he put his head on his pillow, he heard a faint humming noise in his ears.

The Crack in the Pod

. . . CREAK . . .

Mozie pushed open the door and entered the greenhouse. He began to walk immediately—and on purpose this time—to the rear of the greenhouse, where the pod waited behind a screen of leaves.

The vegetables seemed twice as big as they had yesterday. Tomatoes had rolled onto the path, crowded out by other tomatoes. Vines had grown together, and Mozie had to push his way through the thick leaves.

It was like the jungle, and he longed for a machete to

chop his way to the rear of the greenhouse. He did not stop struggling until he was directly in front of the plant.

A little morning sunlight filtered through the leaves, giving the pod a luster, a sheen, which made it seem somehow even more important than it already was.

Mozie glanced from the pod to the deep marks his sneakers and Valvoline's wedgies had left in the soil. He bent and began to smooth them out with his hands. Professor Orloff knew he had seen the pod—he told him that on the phone last night—but Professor Orloff did not know Valvoline had been hugging the pod around the neck and making wishes on its head and wanting to plug it. That thought still caused him to shudder.

When all traces of their scuffling were gone, Mozie sat down on the ledge and leaned back, resting on his elbow. He looked up through the leaves at the pod, squinting a little in the sunlight.

"I'm early because I'm baby-sitting tonight. Batty—he's the guy who usually comes with me—is supposed to baby-sit with me, but he's grounded."

He paused as if giving the pod a chance to respond.

"Oh, yes, Professor Orloff called last night," he went on, speaking directly to the heavy, silent shape above him.

"His presentation has been delayed. You just need to hang on till he gets here. It hasn't helped, of course, that I didn't get the telegram and have been pouring in the Vitagrow."

Mozie sighed and looked down at the dark earth. He

smoothed it idly with one hand. The rich smell did bring visions of the Nile, of ancient tombs, of pyramids older than time, of—Mozie waited for another vision, but that was the extent of his Nile knowledge.

"I guess you heard the thunder last night? I did, and I worried about you. It's going to storm sometime, though, and there will be thunder and lightning . . . Try not to let it get to you."

Mozie got slowly to his feet and brushed off the seat of his pants. The scent of—whatever it was—was so strong, Mozie felt the need of fresh air.

He said, "I'd better leave now."

He turned to go, but something held him in place. He didn't feel that the pod was drawing him closer—it was his own interest. He wanted to lay his head on the pod, to listen to what was going on inside.

Carefully he stepped up onto the ledge. He hesitated only a moment before he pushed the leaves aside and entered the pod's space.

The pod was taller than he was now, and it seemed so heavy Mozie wasn't sure why it didn't fall over. He took one step forward and pressed his ear against the pod in the exact place he had done so yesterday. He heard nothing.

"Are you in there?" he asked. "Are you alive?"

There was nothing.

Mozie put his hands on the pod. His hands were trembling a little. There was no movement, no sound, and yet there was the feeling of energy within the pod. "I know you're not dead," he said. "I bet if Valvoline were here, you'd hum."

He listened again, hoping to hear even the faintest of hums, but there was nothing.

"Well, I'll let you alone."

He stepped back, and as he did, his fingers touched the seam in the pod. He stopped. He pulled back for a better look.

The seam was deeper than it had been yesterday. Mozie remembered how it had looked then. And!

He bent forward. There was a slight crack within the groove. The pod could be getting ready to open.

"Please, please, don't open till Professor Orloff gets back. Please!"

Mozie stepped down from the ledge and started walking backward toward the door. Leaves brushed his back, vines caught at his arms like something in a Disney movie, he stumbled and sat on a basketball-sized tomato. He got up quickly and brushed off the seat of his pants.

"I'll be back tomorrow," he shouted through the foliage. "And you stay closed."

He retreated to the door, turned on the sprinkler system, and left the greenhouse.

Just Mozie

MOZIE RANG the bell. It was one of those old-timey bells that had to be turned.

"Tell my wife to hurry," Mr. Hunter called from the car. "I want to be inside the theater when the storm hits."

Mozie nodded. He rang again.

As the sound jangled in the house, Mozie glanced over his shoulder. The wind was whipping the dry branches of the old magnolia trees. In the distance was a lead wall of clouds, and a gray dome had shot up to thirty thousand feet. The dome turned golden with lightning.

The storm would be here tonight.

As he stood there, Mozie thought of McMummy in the greenhouse. He remembered the faint trembling he and Valvoline had felt as they stood there together with the rich dark smell almost overwhelming them. If she hadn't felt it too, he would have thought it was his imagination, but she had, and he knew that for some reason McMummy feared storms. He wondered if mummies could predict—

From inside the house Mozie heard, "You be a good boy now, Richie, and do what Batty and Mozie tell you."

That'll be the day, Mozie thought. At least he didn't have to bother getting a pleasant look on his face. He already had that, built in—the turned-up nose, turned-up mouth, turned-up eyes, a living, breathing elf.

The heavy oaken door swung open and Mrs. Hunter's face lit up at the sight of him. The only people in the world who were truly delighted to see him, Mozie thought, were Batty and the mothers of unpleasant children. And, so far, the parents with unpleasant children were the only customers for the Macho Baby-Sitters Club.

"Hi, Mrs. Hunter," he said.

She peered out to check the porch. "Where's Batty? I thought he was coming too."

"He's grounded."

"Oh, my, well, at least we've got you."

Dutifully he stepped through the doorway and inhaled the old air of the hall. Years from now, Batty had once told him, scientists would discover that inhaling old air was as bad for your lungs as cigarette smoke.

Batty claimed it would become part of standard health forms:

1. Have you ever smoked?
2. Have you ever inhaled old air?

Mrs. Hunter hugged him, to make up for the old house and the old air and the bad kid in the living room.

"You are so sweet to do this."

Mozie waited out the hug.

"Richie's in the living room. He's been so excited all afternoon. 'What time are they coming? Aren't they here yet?' Go right in."

She turned Mozie in the direction of the living room and started him forward. Like someone in a game of blind man's buff, Mozie moved toward his fate.

"Richie!" Mrs. Hunter called. "Guess what? It's just Mozie, but he's here!"

Mozie and Mrs. Hunter stopped at the sofa, where Richie lay watching TV and sucking his thumb. Mrs. Hunter said, "Richie, look at me." He did this reluctantly. "You are to go to bed at nine o'clock. Don't give Mozie any arguments."

Richie took his thumb out of his mouth, said, "Yes,"

wetly, and put it back in. Mozie knew Richie would promise his mother anything to get her out of the way of the TV.

Mrs. Hunter stepped aside and Richie's eyes refocused.

"If you aren't firm with him, Mozie, he'll keep saying, 'Just five more minutes, just let me watch five more minutes,' until it's six o'clock in the morning."

"Six o'clock! Didn't Mom tell you I have to be home by twelve? I thought you were just going to the movies."

"Oh, we'll be back early." She went to the front door and opened it as quickly as if it were an escape hatch. "You kids have fun," she called as she went out to join Mr Hunter. Mozie moved to the window to watch.

As she opened the car door she said, "It is so good to get out. You just don't know what that son of yours did this morning to my—"

The car door slammed, cutting off the rest of her words.

Mozie lifted his eyes and looked to the horizon. He could see the lightning flashing in the huge cauliflower-like clouds. The tops of those clouds seemed now to reach into the stratosphere. Thunder rumbled in their depths.

Mozie turned from the window and headed for the sofa.

Guinea-Pig Heaven

 "WELL, THEY'RE GONE," Mozie told Richie. He held up his hands like a magician completing a trick. He took a seat on the end cushion. Richie was stretched out on the other two.

"They're off."

Richie did not answer. His eyes stared unblinkingly at the television screen.

"You must like the Dukes."

Mozie felt lonely. He had never before baby-sat alone.

He realized now that Batty was the one who entertained the kids, who made them laugh. He was the silent partner.

He had not wanted to come tonight. All day, with each distant rumble of thunder, he had felt uneasy about the pod. He certainly didn't need the uneasiness of being in charge of a child as well.

Mozie needed someone to talk to, so he said, "They don't do their own stunts though. Batty told me that."

No answer.

"Batty told me another interesting thing. There's this school in California that teaches people to walk on burning coals. This is for real. They walk on red-hot coals and they go, 'Cool moss. Cool moss,' to themselves. Batty can imitate them perfectly. I'll try, but I won't be as funny."

The sound of the phone ringing interrupted him and he got quickly to his feet. "That's probably Batty," he said as he crossed the room.

"Hello."

"Mozie, is that you?"

Mozie recognized Valvoline's voice. "Oh, hi," he said, genuinely pleased.

"Your mom gave me this number. I hope it's all right for me to call when you're baby-sitting. My favorite part of baby-sitting used to be talking on the phone to my friends."

"It's mine too."

"I'll tell you why I'm calling. Do you remember a little

necklace I had on yesterday? It wasn't a necklace—like beads—it was this glass ball that had a mustard seed in it. Mustard seeds bring good luck, in case you didn't know."

"I didn't."

"Well, anyway, I dropped it somewhere, and I've got to find it. I'm going to need all the luck I can get at the pageant. The other contestants can sing and toe dance—one of them is a real ventriloquist—and all I can do is twirl a baton—and half the time I drop that."

"Oh."

"So, I've been thinking back on yesterday, and I'm wondering if when I was jumping around that pod, I might have dropped it."

"I don't think so. I was over there this morning, smoothing out the earth, and I didn't see it."

"Well, will you look again tomorrow?"

"Sure."

"And call me. Your mom has my number."

"I'll call."

"Whether you find it or you don't—I want you to let me know."

"I will, Valvoline."

"I've got to have that seed!"

Mozie hung up the phone and returned to the sofa. A commercial had just come on and Richie sat up. He said, "You know, you know what happened? My guinea pig died."

"Oh, I'm sorry to hear that. I think he was dead when Batty and I were here last time, wasn't he?"

"No."

"Was he sick?"

"No."

"Did he have an accident?"

"No."

"Did you find him?"

"No, I dint."

"Did your mom find him?"

"Yes."

"And he was dead?"

"Yes."

"That's too bad. I never had a guinea pig, but one time I had a hamster. His name was Scrappy, and I know how you feel, because one morning I went in and there was no Scrappy. I went running around the house, going, 'Where's Scrappy? What happened to Scrappy?' I thought he had gotten out of the cage, which he sometimes did, and that Hexic that was our dog's name "

"Gimpy's in guinea-pig heaven."

"Oh." Mozie hesitated, then he said, "I'm not sure there is a guinea-pig heaven, Richie. See, as I understand it—"

"There do too be a guinea-pig heaven!" Richie's hands snapped, soldier quick, to his hips. "My mom said! There be soft grass in guinea-pig heaven and little puddles of water and clean straw for the guinea pigs to sleep on."

"Oh."

"My mom told me all the heavens. Dog heaven has bones and dirt holes already dug under the trees. Cat heaven has bowls of cream and little white mice."

"That wouldn't be heaven for the little mice though, would it?" Mozie said, smiling at his own remark.

Richie didn't seem to like the smile. His hands lifted from his hips to take a boxing stance. He frowned so hard his eyebrows came together. Finally he thought of the answer.

"Little white mice don't go to heaven! They're bad!" To drive home his remark, he started kicking Mozie, hard, his pajamaed feet drumming against Mozie's thigh.

"Stop that! Stop kicking!"

Mozie was already at the end of the sofa, so he couldn't move out of range. He tried to catch one of the feet, but it was like catching a fish.

"I mean it, Richie. I don't like to be kicked. If you keep on kicking, I'm going to turn off the TV. I mean it. If you kick me one more time . . . All right. That's it! The TV goes off! *O-F-F*. Off!"

Mozie darted to the television and clicked it off. This action made him feel enormously better. He was in control after all.

There was a moment of stunned silence and then a wail that went all the way to the roof.

"My mom said I could watch till nine o'clock. You big

dum-dum, you." Richie came off the sofa with his hands made into fists.

Mozie turned sideways like somebody in a bullring and then moved back as Richie punched his way to the TV. Richie's fists were lashing out, kung fu style.

Mozie moved behind an easy chair.

Richie stabbed the TV back on, glared at Mozie, and went back to the sofa.

He shook his fist at Mozie as he lay down. "And leave it like that, dum-dum!"

Mozie wanted to throw back his head and howl with helplessness. He couldn't help McMummy, he couldn't help himself—his thoughts broke off as the wind began whistling around the house—and he couldn't stop the storm.

Behind the Beanstalk

TO TAKE HIS MIND off his worries, Mozie was coloring a picture in Richie's coloring book.

Mozie had not colored in years, had never actually been much of a colorer, and so he was now surprised that he had opened the book—*Jumbo Fairy-Tale Fun,* two hundred pages of pictures, puzzles, and games—and was totally engrossed in coloring a picture of Jack and the beanstalk.

He had always liked the story of Jack and his widowed

mother fending for themselves. They were, it seemed to Mozie, the only real characters in the whole of fairyland. He had at first wanted to color a picture of Jack and his mother at the cottage door, with the mother's arms outstretched to welcome him home, but he had decided on a picture of the enormous vine with Jack ascending through the leaves.

It was eight o'clock, and Mozie had been working on the picture for fifteen minutes, growing more and more pleased as he colored each leaf perfectly. The huge vine seemed to be coming to life on the page.

He drew back to admire his artistry. Then he selected a brown crayon from the stubs in the cigar box. Mozie was used to twenty-four perfect Crayolas, and this cigar box had held these stubs for so long the inside was dark with crayon marks.

Even with these imperfect crayons, he was doing a sensational job. He started on the stem. He began humming.

"You went out of the line," Richie said at his shoulder.

"I did not."

"You did too."

"I did not. Where?"

"Right here."

Mozie bent over the page. He had somehow colored between two leaves, and this had formed a sort of shadowy figure. "I did that on purpose. I wanted to give the effect of something behind the leaves."

"Uh-uh! You went out of the li-ine. You went out of the li-ine. You went out of the—"

Mozie let the coloring book fall to his lap. "All right, all right. I went out of the line."

He leaned back against the sofa and closed his eyes. Going out of the line on Jack's bean plant suddenly depressed him. He felt so bad that he wondered if a mental illness could start this way.

He would see the school counselor in the fall. Mr. Franklin would go, "Of course you can talk to me, Mozie. You students are always welcome to talk over your problems. What is it, exactly, that you're depressed about?"

"You'll think it's nothing, Mr. Franklin."

"No, no. Sometimes these little problems turn into big ones. It's easier to deal with them before that time."

He'd hesitate.

"You can tell me anything, Mozie."

"Well, all right. I went out of the line on Jack's bean plant."

He could feel Richie's warm breath on his cheek. Richie was inches away, peering into his face. Mozie did not open his eyes. "It's rude to stare at people," he said.

Richie said, "What was behind the plant?"

"Nothing."

"You said something was behind the plant."

"I don't know."

"You have to know because you said it."

"I really don't know."

"A monster?"

Mozie felt a chill on the back of his neck.

"There's no such thing as monsters."

"There do too be monsters."

"There—are—no—monsters."

"In the ground there be monsters."

"No."

"My friend Michael told me. They curl up down there. One time, one time we were digging and Michael's shovel hit a monster and we had to run in the house before it got us."

Mozie clamped his lips together and said nothing.

"Anyway, it be all right to go out of the line. I go out of the line a lot."

Richie sounded so sorry that Mozie wondered if he had at last managed to look depressed. He would have to remember this moment, the way an actor remembers a personal experience to get a certain expression. For the rest of his life, anytime he needed to look depressed, he could remember the time he went out of the line on Jack's bean plant. At funerals, at sad plays, when Batty wouldn't baby-sit with him—

There was a trio of computer notes on the television and Mozie opened his eyes. The station played these notes when some sort of warning was going to be announced—a bad storm or no school or—

"You can color another picture," Richie said in his contrite voice.

"Shut up, Richie, I want to hear this."

"A line of severe thunderstorms is moving toward the following counties: Mecklenburg, Oconee, Columbia, Winterdale, Downs—"

"That's us—Downs," Mozie said.

"Hail and lightning and strong winds are associated with this line of storms. Winds gusting to forty miles an hour—"

"You can color the whole book if you want to."

"Shut up, Richie."

Mozie leaned forward on the sofa, his body stiff with alarm.

Richie said, "It not be nice to say shut up."

"Shut up! Here comes the bulletin across the bottom of the screen again. Oh, this is a new one: 'A tornado watch has been issued until ten o'clock for the following counties—'

"See, that's something new. Tornadoes."

The same bulletin repeated, but Mozie watched it as intently as if he had never seen it before. These bulletins had become an instant addiction.

"Why did you say shut up?"

"Because I want to see this on TV."

"Why do you want to see this on TV?"

"Because a storm warning is on."

"Why is a storm warning on?"

"Because!"

Concern made his voice unnaturally high. He took a deep breath. The last thing he wanted to do was to alarm Richie, but this talk of monsters, this strange appearance of a pod behind Jack's bean plant—it was beginning to get to him.

In a voice so soft and modulated it could have come from *Mr. Rogers' Neighborhood,* he said, "I want to see this because I want to know about storms."

Mozie heard the sound of a car on the road. He said quickly, "Someone's coming! Maybe your mom and dad heard about the storm!"

He got to his feet and ran to the window.

The car did not turn into the driveway. It passed by and began to build up speed for the hill ahead.

Mozie sighed. Then he raised his head and looked beyond the road, to the mountains. He could see the lightning flashing in the sky, turning the sky white. The thunder boomed.

"It's coming," he said.

"What did you say?" Richie asked from the sofa.

"Nothing. I was talking to myself."

"You can't talk to yourself because I be here. If I be here you have to be talking to me."

"All right, I was talking to you."

"So, so what did you say to me?"

"It's coming," Mozie answered.

The Storm

MOZIE WAS SITTING on the sofa with Richie on his lap. They had been like this for thirty minutes, waiting for the storm to hit. Mozie's legs were getting numb.

"Want to lie down for a minute, Richie?"

"Noooo. Don't put me dowwwwnnnnn!"

"But the storm's still miles away. Listen, see, there's the lightning, now listen to me count—one-thousand-and-one, one-thousand-and-two, one-thousand-and-three, one-thousand-and-four. Now, there's the thunder. The storm's four miles away."

"Do four miles be a lot?"

"Yes."

"It dint sound like a lot."

"Well, it is."

"Don't put me dowwwnnnn!"

Mozie sighed. He realized he could never be a department-store Santa Claus—even though he had the face for it—because he could not hold children on his lap without wanting to let them slide off. "Whoops, old Santa's so sorry. Whoops, dropped you again, did I? How 'bout that. Old Santa's . . . "

The wind was getting stronger. It was beginning to whine around the chimney. Mozie could hear the branches of the magnolia trees whipping together. An occasional limb was blown off a tree and struck the house.

Mozie said, "Richie, I have to make one very short phone call. I want to speak to my mom. She doesn't watch TV and she may not know about this storm. I'll leave you for one minute—here's my watch." He slipped off his watch. Richie took it and threw it on the floor.

With a sigh, Mozie made an effort to retrieve his watch and keep Richie from slipping off his lap.

"Richie, now listen. I've got to call my mom."

"Take me with you."

"To the phone?"

"Yes."

"It's just right over there. You can see me the whole time."

"I want to go with you."

"I don't think I can, Richie. You're a big boy."

"No, I be little."

"Why, I think you're a big boy. I think—"

"Waahhhhhhhhh—"

"Well, maybe I can," Mozie said. "I'll give it a try."

Mozie struggled to his feet, holding Richie in his arms as if he were a baby. Richie began sagging in the middle, so Mozie pushed him higher with one knee.

"This isn't going to work. Let's try piggyback."

As he was helping Richie onto his back, the phone began to ring. "Oh, there's the phone. It's Mom!"

He hurried toward the phone sideways, like a crab, with Richie on one hip. He picked up the receiver.

"Mom!"

Batty's voice said, "I can't talk but a minute. This storm is coming—I just heard it on TV—with dangerous hail— hail! You know what hail can do to a greenhouse? It's—"

"I know about the storm. I know about the hail. I thought you were going to be my mother." With great control he stopped himself from yelling, "I want my mother!"

"Also tornadoes—which probably won't actually hap- pen—but hail—the TV said golf ball–sized hail to baseball-sized hail. You know what golf ball–sized hail can do to a greenhouse?"

"Yes."

"It can shatter every pane of glass, batter every plant. Do you remember the time I hit a baseball through someone's picture window?"

"That was our picture window."

"Well, remember—" He broke off. "I got to go. Linda's coming."

The conversation ended with a bang. Mozie waited a moment and then hung up the phone.

"Was that Batty?" Richie asked.

"Yes."

"I wish Batty was here instead of you."

"So do I."

"Batty makes me laugh."

"He makes me laugh too."

Mozie picked up the phone again and dialed his own number. He waited for fourteen rings, but there was no answer at Crumb Castle. "Where can she be? She can't be out in the storm." He dialed again. Again no answer.

As he put down the phone, he heard the sound of rain— big drops—they had to be as big as golf balls themselves— begin to pelt the roof like bullets. The wind grew stronger. Lightning struck close by with an ear-splitting crash. The air had a strange metallic smell.

Richie clutched Mozie around the neck.

"Not so hard. You're strangling me." Mozie began to make his way back to the sofa. "Let go of my neck, or I'm going to—"

This was his big weakness as a baby-sitter, one of his big weaknesses—he didn't know how to make kids do things they didn't want to do. The only thing he could think of— I'm going to take you to the doctor and tell him to give you a shot—wouldn't work because Richie knew Mozie didn't have wheels.

"Noooooooooooooooooo—"

"Let go, I'm not kidding."

A shutter on an upstairs window began to bang against the house. The porch swing began to do the same thing. A limb crashed onto the porch.

There was a blinding flash of lightning.

"One-thousand-and-one, one-thousand-and-two," Mozie counted in an unsteady voice.

Then came the thunder. Two miles away that time.

The huge drops of rain on the roof sounded louder now, as if frozen. Hail.

Then there came a crash of lightning so loud, so earsplitting, so powerful that the floor actually shook under Mozie's feet.

And the lights went out.

Thunder and Lightning

IN THE DARK LIVING ROOM Mozie held Richie on his lap while the storm raged. He had stopped having cheerful thoughts about Santa dropping kids on the floor. Mozie was afraid.

The black, almost primordial darkness of the room was broken by blinding flashes of white lightning. There was no separation between the thunder and lightning now.

Richie had a cushion over his ears. Mozie wanted to hold one over his head too, but every time he loosened his grip on Richie, Richie began to scream.

The house had started to shake with the fury of the storm. Doors rattled. Windows trembled so hard that glass panes popped and splintered into the house. The thunder overhead was like tons of stones falling on the house.

"Do you have a basement?" Mozie said.

Richie didn't hear him.

Mozie picked up one side of the pillow. "Do you have a basement? If you do, we ought to get down in it."

"I don't know."

"You have to know if you have a basement!"

"What be a basement?"

At that moment, the door to the garage burst open and the storm was in the house. Curtains flew in the air. Rain splattered into the kitchen, a lamp blew over in the bedroom.

A scream rose in Mozie's throat and he struggled to his feet. He would have dropped Richie if Richie had not gotten another of those strangleholds around his neck.

"It's us," Mrs. Hunter called. She was out of breath. "We're back."

She held a flashlight under her chin to prove her identity, but a blinding flash of lightning turned her into a stranger and made Mozie want to scream more than ever.

"Mommy, Mommy," Richie cried. He pushed his way out of Mozie's arms and ran for his mother.

"It's all right," she told him. She looked at Mozie. "The power is off all over town. Lines are down. The Hawkinses' whole pecan grove—every single tree—is laid over on its side. We saw fire trucks turning in to the"—she broke off as the thunder rattled the house—"the airport," she finished.

She took off her scarf with her free hand and shook the drops of water from it. "I've never seen such a mess."

In his mother's arms, Richie said, "Mozie told me to shut up."

Mozie came forward tensely. "Where's Mr. Hunter?"

"Trying to get the garage doors shut."

"Why? Isn't he going to drive me home?"

"There is no way you can get home tonight. We'll call your mother—if the phone isn't out. Lines are down all over town. We had to drive to Sumpter to get home."

"But my mom's expecting me. If I'm not there . . . "

"Your mother will know you can't get home."

"But I could if Mr. Hunter would drive me!"

"That's not possible, Mozie."

Mozie's shoulders slumped.

"Now, now," Mrs. Hunter gave him one of her hugs. "You can sleep in the guest room. I'll get one of Bob's T-shirts for you to sleep in, and in the morning"—another hug—"in the morning Bob will drive you home."

"I'll walk," Mozie said.

"Absolutely not. I won't hear of your walking."

"I don't mind."

"Well, I do."

"I want to walk."

"You are not leaving this house. Bob, talk to him."

Mr. Hunter was closing the door to the kitchen, and Mrs. Hunter swung the flashlight around to spotlight him. "Bob, he has some idea that he can get home tonight. He's talking about walking!"

"No," Mr. Hunter said, shaking his head. "There are trees blocking the roads. Power lines are down. It's like a war zone out there."

"See?" Mrs. Hunter said. "Now, come on, Richie, I want you in bed. And Mozie, I know you're tired too."

Reluctantly Mozie allowed himself to be pushed down the hall. Mrs. Hunter opened a door and shone the flashlight, revealing a room that appeared never to have been used.

"I'll leave this flashlight with you," she said. "Bob's getting some candles for us."

Mr. Hunter came down the hall, lighting his way with a candle. "Here's the T-shirt."

"And there are toothbrushes in the guest bathroom. What we all need now is a good night's sleep." She lifted her head. "The storm is moving on—listen!"

"If it's moving on—" Mozie began quickly, but Mrs. Hunter cut off his words by giving him a hug.

Mozie was still standing in the hall, keeping his toes out of the guest room the way Batty kept his toes out of his sister's bedroom when he had to talk to her for some reason.

"Well, go on in." Mrs. Hunter gave him a gentle shove, put the flashlight in his hand, and Mozie, much against his will, found himself for the first time in his life in a guest bedroom.

Daddy Longlegs

MOZIE LAY STIFFLY on the guest bed. He had taken all of the little pillows off and put them on a chair, but he was still uncomfortable. The remaining pillow had lace on it.

Mozie felt stiff and awkward and strange. More than anything in the world, he wanted to be home.

He shifted. He was wearing Mr. Hunter's T-shirt, but his legs were cold. He didn't want to get under the covers because the sheets had lace on them too.

If he were at home, he thought, and if he felt this strange and uncomfortable, he would know exactly what to do. He would get out of bed, go to his closet, and take his father's box down from the top shelf. The box on the shelf in his closet and its contents were the only valuable, irreplaceable things Mozie had ever owned.

He would sit with the box on his lap and he would lift the lid. And always, there would be the immediate smell of leather and wool and a vague, indefinably masculine scent—after-shave perhaps. What Mozie knew of after-shave he had learned in Eckerds, standing in men's toiletries, testing the various scents, but he was never able to identify the exact one that his father had favored. Perhaps his father had shopped at a finer store.

At any rate, the sum total was the true scent of his father. Mozie had no actual memory of his father—he had died when Mozie was a baby—but when he opened this box, he got a sense of his father that was strong and loving. It never failed to comfort Mozie.

Everything in this box had belonged to his father, had been worn by him or used by him or saved by him. On top was his dad's wallet—leather, dark and smooth. His father had worn his wallet in his hip pocket, his mom had told Mozie, and so it still bore the slight curve of the contour of his body.

Inside the wallet he could see his father's face, framed in

a yellow construction hard hat. His eyes were bright and brown, kind eyes. Mozie would flip slowly through the wallet, checking the other IDs, the credit cards, the snapshot of his mother, the lock of her hair curled in one corner. Among the contents of the box was a Swiss army knife, and one blade of that knife was the tiny scissors his father had used to cut the curl from his mother's neck.

Mozie liked that story, but his favorite was how his parents met. They met at an Elks dance. The first time his mom saw his dad he was sitting down at a table. He was the same medium height as everyone else.

He asked her to dance and she said, "Yes." They stood up together, and Mozie's father was the tallest man she had ever seen off a basketball court. "His legs! His legs! I fell in love with your dad because of his legs!" she always cried in such a comical way that Mozie begged to hear the story again and again. "Tell about Daddy's long legs," he'd say.

Later his mom told Mozie she had once read a book called *Daddy-Long-Legs,* and they checked it out of the library and read it together. After that, their nickname for him was Daddy Longlegs.

Mozie would give a lot right now to be sitting on his own bed, turning through his dad's wallet, touching the dollar bills, the exact ones that had been in his wallet the day his dad died, saying to himself that his father had touched this ten-dollar bill, this five, these very ones that he was touching.

Mozie got out of bed. He walked to the window. The moon was full and beautiful and the air was so clear it seemed that the moon was within reach.

In the bright moonlight, Mozie could see the destruction. The Hunters' yard was covered with branches from trees, big branches. Hail, big as eggs, shone white against the ground. The driveway was completely blocked by the wreckage.

And what had the Hunters said about the airport? Fire trucks had turned into the airport? Crumb Castle was right at the end of runway 28. And the greenhouse was not two miles away.

He began to tremble. He knew the greenhouse had not survived—the wind would have blown out the glass panes if the hail had not shattered them. And the limbs from the forest . . . And if none of that happened—if the greenhouse still stood, there had been thunder—the thunder so dreaded by the pod that it trembled at the sound.

Now his mind traveled to the thought he had been avoiding. His own house . . . Crumb Castle . . . his mother.

With a heavy heart, Mozie crossed to the guest bed. He wished he could cry, but he had never been much of a crier. Even as a baby he had cried so seldom that his mother had asked the doctor if he were normal.

He wanted to cry. The unshed tears were an actual, physical ache.

He lay down.

It was just as well, he told himself. He would have gotten tears on the guest-room sheets.

Greenhouse

 "THE GOOD THING about the storm is that it finally got me out of the house," Batty said, "only I'm sort of on parole. Whatever you do, don't ever make me laugh at my sister's piano playing again."

Batty and Mozie were picking their way through the forest, on their way to the greenhouse. They worked their way around a fallen tree.

Over the weeks that Mozie had been taking care of the greenhouse, he had worn a path through the trees. Now the path was so littered with the effects of the storm that it had disappeared.

"I had 'stick and limb' duty this morning," Batty continued. "There were sticks and branches all over the place, and so after my dad and I cleaned up the whole yard, then my mother agreed I could come over and help you—since you don't have a dad to do that kind of thing."

Mozie did not reply. The closer they got to the greenhouse, the more his dread of seeing it grew. This was what his life had consisted of for the last few days—a feeling of dread interrupted by feelings of sorrow, despair, fear, even joy. But the dread was always there, returning in a rush as soon as the other emotions receded.

The one moment of joy had come when he and Mr. Hunter drove up to Crumb Castle at noon. Mozie had been up at dawn, but Mr. Hunter refused to leave until he heard on the radio that the streets were cleared.

They turned into Crumb Castle's drive and Mozie saw his mom standing in the front yard with a tree limb in her hand, as if she were wondering what to do with it. Her face looked worried, but the lines smoothed out into absolute, total happiness as she saw Mozie's face looking out of the window of Mr. Hunter's car. She dropped the limb and held out her arms as Jack's mother had in the picture he almost colored.

"I've been so worried," she had said, running across the

yard to embrace him. Pine Cone was at her heels, as if he didn't want to risk separation.

Mr. Hunter got out of the car to explain about the guest room and the trees being down on Sumpter Road while Mozie remained in his mother's arms, for once not twisting with embarrassment to get away. Pine Cone rubbed around the back of his legs.

But then, as soon as Mr. Hunter drove away, and he and his mother began to clean the yard of Crumb Castle, the thought of the greenhouse returned . . . and the dread.

If there had been this much damage to their trees, he thought, the greenhouse could not have escaped unharmed.

"I'll have to go check the greenhouse, Mom. It's probably ruined."

"You don't have to go right now. There's nothing you can do, Mozie."

"There might be."

"I haven't let myself think about that greenhouse."

"I thought of it all night."

"Well, it's just plants. Plants can be replaced. Human beings can't."

"But—"

"You and I are alive and well—and, Mozie—" She took him by the shoulders and turned him to her. She looked into his face. "That's not true of everybody in this county. That trailer court behind the laundry is wiped off the face of the earth. I hear there are whole airplanes up in the trees at the airport. Mrs. Miller told me—"

Her list of dooms was interrupted by a triumphant yell from the street, and they turned to see Batty arriving on his bicycle. For once he looked more cheerful than Mozie.

"I'm free!" he cried, coming to a stop on the slick grass.

"Good." Mrs. Mozer turned to Mozie. "Now Batty can go with you to the greenhouse. That way it won't seem so bad if it's damaged."

"I want to go, Mrs. Mozer," Batty said. "I wouldn't miss it for anything."

But now, as they neared the greenhouse, Batty was speaking less positively. "If the greenhouse has been destroyed—I mean, I hope it hasn't—"

"It has," Mozie interrupted with flat certainty.

"Well, if it *has* been destroyed, then . . . "

"Then what?" Mozie prompted.

"Then let's cut the pod open and see what was inside," Batty finished in a rush.

Mozie gave his friend a look—not *the* look, but a look of displeasure—but Batty didn't notice. "I cannot spend the rest of my life wondering what was inside that pod!" Batty said.

"Well, I want to know too . . . "

"Then let's do it. If it's dead—it'll be like an autopsy on TV. We'll be doing mankind a favor."

As they stepped into the clearing, they both fell silent. The greenhouse lay before them in total ruin.

The wind seemed to have hit the greenhouse broadside, sweeping broken glass and plants into the forest, and the hail had done the rest. Vegetables were smashed into pulp, mashed so badly that there was no telling what they had once been.

The pipe that connected the sprinkler system had burst, and a fountain of water shot, geyserlike, into the air. Gradually it washed the debris deeper into the forest.

Shards of glass were everywhere, and the drops of water trapped beneath gave the impression the boys were approaching a lake of ice.

Glass crunched beneath their feet as they walked forward, and Mozie felt as if he were walking into a nightmare.

They paused at the edge of the geyser's reach. Batty gave a low whistle. "Yesterday this was a regular greenhouse," he said, "with plants that could save the world."

"I know," Mozie answered, remembering the last time he had seen it.

"They're calling it a killer storm and they're right. I'm going this way."

Batty headed for the rear of the greenhouse, skirting the worst of the damage. Mozie followed.

"That's the plant," Mozie said, looking at what had once been a corner of the greenhouse.

Batty stopped beside him.

The roots of the huge plant had been pulled from the soft earth, and the plant itself—or what was left of it—lay on its side, toppled. Mozie thought of the picture in Richie's coloring book where that vine lay dying on the ground.

Stripped of its leaves, the stem seemed fragile. It had been severed in places and a dark brown pulp showed through the pale green of the outside.

Batty circled the plant. "But where's the pod?" he asked.

"Probably ruined."

"Yes, ruined, but where are the ruins? There has to be something left."

"Maybe it's so smashed . . . "

"I'm not leaving here until I see it—smashed or not," Batty said.

The Empty
Birthday Present

MOZIE AND BATTY separated and began crisscrossing the damaged area. Mozie felt he had entered a place not of this earth. Once he thought he heard the faint hum of an airplane engine and he looked up, but the sky was clear.

The boys stepped over fallen girders, slid on the smashed vegetables, picked up huge wilted leaves to look underneath.

Batty slipped and went down on one knee. He said, "This makes me sick," as he got up. "That's got to be squash," he said, pointing to his pants. "I can't stand the stuff. And isn't this smell getting to you?"

"Yes, I'm ready to go home," Mozie said tiredly. "I didn't sleep at all, Batty. I was in the Hunters' guest room."

"I hate them things," Batty said. "But I am not leaving until I see the pod."

Mozie sighed. "What am I going to tell the professor?"

"Don't tell him anything. Save the newspapers, and when he gets home . . . " Batty broke off. "Wait a minute. Wait a minute. Wait a minute." He began walking faster over the broken glass.

"What?"

"Wait a minute!"

"What?" Mozie began to follow.

At the edge of the woods, Batty paused. "There it is! I knew that was it! There—it—is!"

The pod lay just at the edge of the forest, out of the destruction. It had not been damaged by hail or glass—its surface was unmarked except for the tree that lay across it, crushing it and pinning it to the ground.

Mozie and Batty stood side by side, shoulders touching. Neither of them moved.

Batty had not moved out of respect for the dead—something he had learned from TV cop shows. Mozie had not moved because he felt terrible.

"It almost—almost got away," Batty said. "If that tree hadn't . . . "

"What do you mean—got away?"

"I don't know what I mean. It just looked like it was almost into the forest, where there was protection from the hail. We got to get this tree out of the way so we can operate."

The tree was not a large one, but it lay across the middle of the pod. Lightning had splintered its trunk into pieces, and Batty began pulling at the loose wood.

"This could take a month," he said. He put his hands on the pod and pressed.

"What are you doing?"

"If we could press it down, we could slip it out from under the tree. But this thing is hard, and it's as big as a mattress."

Batty took the stem of the pod and pulled. It did not come loose. "We are never going to get inside this thing."

"I know."

"We got to have a knife," Batty said. "Go get the biggest knife—"

"My mom doesn't let me play with knives," Mozie said.

"This isn't play. This is the opposite of play. This is the hardest work we're ever going to do in our lives."

Mozie started reluctantly back to the house. His mother was at her sewing machine—that was good. He entered the kitchen, opened the knife drawer, and took out the butcher knife.

His mother always had a special sense about the opening of the knife drawer. "No knives," she called.

"Batty and I have to cut something. A tree fell on something and we've got to cut it."

"No knives! I don't like you playing with my knives."

Mozie hesitated a moment and then he ran upstairs. He took the box from his closet—the box containing his father's belongings. He lifted the lid, not pausing now to be comforted by the scent.

He reached into the box and brought up his father's Swiss army knife. Without bothering to close the box, he rushed down the stairs and out the door.

He ran through the forest and to the clearing where the ruined greenhouse lay.

Batty was kneeling on the pod, peering through a crack. "I'm trying to tear it open," he said, "but this stuff is like leather or rubber or something that won't tear and won't chip. I sure hope it cuts. Give me the knife."

Mozie took his father's knife from his pocket. "Give it here," Batty said.

"It's my knife. I get to use it."

"Well, use it then."

Mozie knelt beside the pod. He pulled out a blade that turned out to be the little scissors. He put it back. He pulled out the toothpick. He put it back.

Batty snorted with impatience.

This time Mozie brought out the sharpest blade. He bent over the pod. "Right over the heart," Batty suggested.

Mozie nodded. He swallowed and he pressed the blade

into the thick green covering. It resisted. He lifted the blade and stabbed lightly at the pod.

"Hard!" Batty said. He was at Mozie's side, giving stabbing movements of his own.

"I don't want to hurt it."

"It's dead! Give me the knife."

"I'll do it!"

Mozie lifted the knife high and brought it down on the pod. It entered with a wet noise, and liquid oozed out around the blade.

"That's more like it," Batty said.

Now Mozie began to cut an opening in the pod. It was slow going—like opening a can with a knife—and several times he paused. At each pause, Batty would say, "Want me to have a turn?" Mozie would shake his head and continue.

A half hour passed, and Mozie was at last completing his circle. He cut the last inch and paused as if he had expected the circle to fall into the pod.

"Lift it out," Batty said.

Mozie tried to pull it out with his fingertips.

"No, with the knife, give me the knife."

At last he surrendered the knife to Batty. "Like this," Batty said. He stabbed the center of the circle lightly and withdrew the circle.

It flopped over onto the pod and then slid to the ground with a wet plop.

Batty and Mozie leaned forward together to peer through the small circle. "Me first," Mozie said. He had waited a long time for this. He put one hand on either side of the hole, claiming it for himself.

Batty shrugged and pulled back. Mozie bent his face to the circle. There was a smell so heady Mozie thought he would faint.

He looked and pulled back.

"What is it? What? Let me look, will you?"

Mozie gestured to the hole and stepped back. "At last," Batty said. He leaned forward, one hand braced on either side of the pod. He gasped.

"It's empty. We've been robbed!"

Mozie nodded.

Batty took another, longer look. "Empty!" he said. "Hello! Anybody in there?" Batty rapped on the pod. "Knock knock. Who's there? No. No who? No body." He laughed at his own joke. He glanced back at Mozie. "I wonder if this is the way doctors act in the operating room when they cut a hole in somebody's chest."

"I hope not."

Batty rested his weight against the pod. "Do you know what this means?" he asked thoughtfully.

Mozie couldn't answer.

"This means that whatever was inside the pod got out."

Mozie couldn't answer.

"And if it got out, it can move."

Mozie couldn't answer. He wasn't sure he would ever speak again.

"And if it can move, it's alive." Batty glanced over his shoulder at Mozie. "Let's look for it, want to? Footprints! Look for footprints! We'll track it down. Like Bigfoot." Batty began circling the ruined pod. "Footprints. There have to be footprints . . . unless . . . " Batty's shoulders sagged.

"Unless what, Bat?"

"Unless it was empty all the time."

"I don't think it was."

"You know what this reminds me of? One time Benny Rogers—"

"I don't think it was."

"Let me finish. One time Benny Rogers came to my birthday party and I opened his present and the box was empty. Empty! Do you know what it feels like to open an empty birthday present?

"Later Benny's mom explained that Benny's little brother had taken my gift out to play with it and Benny's mom didn't know this and she wrapped up the box and sent Benny to the party. But can you imagine what it feels like to open an empty birthday present?"

He stretched out his arms to take in the pod.

"It feels exactly like this!"

Missing McMummy

 THIS TIME when Mozie's mother awakened him in the middle of the night, Mozie knew what had happened.

"The professor," he said.

"Yes."

"I don't want to talk to him, Mom. He'll yell at me about the greenhouse being destroyed."

"That wasn't your fault."

"I know, but—"

"You want me to tell him?"

He hesitated and sighed. "No, I'll do it."

He got up tiredly and padded barefooted to his mother's bedroom. He picked up the phone.

"Hello," he said.

"Howard Mozer?" It was the operator.

"Yes."

"Go ahead, Professor Orloff, your party is on the line."

"Allo! Allo! Are you there?"

"Yes," said Mozie, "but something terrible's happened."

"No, iss not terrible, iss goot. The congress has accepted my proposal. Dey are prowiding me vith a huge greenhouse—huge, Hovard. I will grow wegetables for the vorld!"

"But your wegetables here . . . " Mozie began. He started over. "Professor, there was a storm—a killer storm, the newspapers are calling it."

"Ya?"

"And McMummy is missing."

"Vat? Vat iss missing?"

"The mummy pod. The pod! Remember I told you that there was a huge pod on one of the plants?"

"Ya?"

"Well, that pod is missing. I mean, the pod's not missing, but what was inside it is missing."

"Somevun stole the beans?"

"If that was what was inside."

"Vat vas inside novun knows." He paused. "But dey haff a goot meal, ya?"

The professor's laughter boomed into the telephone at his joke. Mozie grimaced.

His mother said, "Find out when he's coming back, Mozie."

"Professor, when are you coming back?"

"I am not returning. De greenhouse is yours. Do vit it vat you—"

"I don't want the greenhouse. It's ruined. It's—"

"It served its purpose. I am hanging up now. I meet my challenge. I prowide the vorld vith vegetables! Goot-bye! Goot-bye!"

The phone went dead, and Mozie stood for a moment as if in shock. He looked up at his mother. "He isn't coming back."

"At least he paid you in advance," his mother said, trying to smile.

Mozie nodded. He started for his room and paused in the doorway with his back to his mother.

"Did you hear what I said about the pod being empty?"

"Yes."

"Well, Professor Orloff made a joke of it. He said someone stole the beans. But, Mom—please don't laugh when I tell you this. I can't stand it if you laugh."

"I won't."

"Batty and I found the pod this afternoon. It was crushed by a tree, but it was whole."

"Go on," his mother said when he paused.

"So we were going to cut it open—that's why I wanted the butcher knife. I got Dad's army knife and we cut a circle and looked inside and it was empty."

"And?"

"And Batty thinks it was empty all along, but I don't. Later I went back and I put my hand inside, and I could feel—well, ridges like, here and here."

He pointed to the space between his arms and chest. "And I reached up and there was a narrowing, like for a neck, and then it widened as if for a head."

He was still facing into the hallway.

"And I took my knife and I went around the whole upper half and I lifted it up—it was like lifting up the half-lid of a coffin. And in the case was—what it had felt like—the shape of a person "

"Mozie."

"What?"

"I don't want you to go back to that greenhouse."

"I might have to."

"You don't have to do anything. I wish now I'd never let you go in the first place. Look at me, Mozie."

He turned.

"I don't know if I can explain this, but a person can get so caught up in things—and I do this myself—so caught up in things that—"

She broke off. He could see she was having trouble expressing herself. That was a trait that they shared.

"Like last year I was in the mall," she continued, but she was still struggling with what she had to say, "and there was a lot of noise, but over all that noise, as clear as I hear my own voice right now, I heard your father's voice call, 'Lily!'

"And I turned around and I expected to see him and when I didn't see him, I was almost physically sick with disappointment. I could hardly drive home. Mozie, the imagination is a powerful, powerful force."

He felt almost sick himself, but he said stubbornly, "I'm not imagining."

She straightened. "Then that is all the more reason to stay away from the greenhouse."

They watched each other for a moment. His mother was looking into his eyes as hard as if she were trying to see what was going on behind them.

She turned her eyes to the ceiling. She seemed to be reaching for some other argument. But when she looked back, she sighed. "Well, let's go to bed. We can hash this out in the morning. Good night, Mozie."

"Good night."

Hummmmm

 "I'VE COME for my dress," Valvoline said. She spun into Crumb Castle.

Mrs. Mozer said, "I guess you'll want to try it on."

"Yes! I can't wait to see myself in it."

Mozie said quickly, "I'll be in the kitchen."

Mozie's mother brought out the dress on a hanger. Mozie went through the kitchen and onto the back steps. He sat down. Pine Cone came out of the bushes and rubbed against his legs. Pine Cone had been very friendly since the storm.

"Ah, Pine," he said. He put his hand on the cat's side and felt the comfortable purr.

Inside his mother said, "Now, aren't you glad you didn't have me take it in? It fits perfectly."

"Hold the mirror so I can see the back." There was a pause, then an explosion of pleasure. "I love it. I love it. I want to show Mozie. Mozie, where are you?"

"I'm here," he said, getting to his feet.

Valvoline swirled onto the back porch, creating a small eddy of sweet-scented air. Mozie's head snapped up and his mouth opened.

Valvoline was the most beautiful thing he had ever seen. She was radiant.

"Am I going to win or am I going to win?"

"Oh, you'll win, all right."

"I wish you were one of the judges." She started back into the house, then turned. "Are you coming? Please—to cheer for me."

Mozie hesitated.

"Your mom promised she'd come."

"Oh, all right."

"I'd hug you if I didn't have on this beautiful, exhilarating, fascinating, pageant-winning dress!"

She disappeared into the house. Pine Cone came back for the last half of his neck rub. Mozie put his hand on Pine Cone's side. He felt the deep humming, the purring.

Valvoline's perfume hung in the still summer air.

Pine Cone's purr grew louder. "Wow, you really are happy," Mozie said, and then he realized the faint hum was not coming just from the cat.

He shook his head to clear it. This humming had been recurring in his mind since that moment when he had stood in the scented bower and first heard it. He imagined this was because that was the moment he became aware of things beyond his understanding, things alien to all he knew, a world where anything could happen.

Valvoline went out the front door and called, "See you at the pageant," to Mozie. Mozie walked slowly around the house to watch her back out of the drive.

The hum was stronger now. It seemed to be coming from the woods.

Mozie stood without moving. Pine Cone came to join him and then stopped. The hair rose on Pine Cone's back. Pine Cone let out a low yowling sound.

Mozie bent to pat him. "What's wrong, Pine Cone? I'm not leaving. I'm just . . . "

Eyes wide, Pine Cone turned and ran for the house. Mozie could hear him scratching on the screen, begging to be let in.

Mozie didn't have time for the cat. Already the sound was fading. He started toward the woods.

Mozie located the direction of the humming sound and quickened his pace. He broke into a run. He crossed the yard. At the edge of the forest, he paused. He listened.

Overhead a plane droned in the pattern for runway 28, blocking out the sound.

Mozie moved into the forest, slowly, stepping around the remnants of the storm. As he came to a fallen tree, he paused again.

The plane had landed, its engine no longer interfering with the hum. Mozie listened. A bird called somewhere in the forest. A woodpecker worked on a limb. But the humming sound was gone.

As Mozie turned to go back to the house, he glanced down and stopped. He saw something that did not quite fit. He had almost missed it. He would have if the sunlight hadn't been shining on it. Slowly he dropped to his knees.

There, against the protruding limb of the fallen tree, was a scrap of green. In the sunlight that filtered through the trees it seemed to shimmer with a light of its own.

Mozie reached out and took the scrap of green in his hand. It lay on his palm, as delicate as a butterfly wing, thin as tissue paper. Drops of moisture, tiny beads, came from the torn end of the scrap.

Mozie drew in his breath. He had the feeling that he was the first person in the world to see this. He got to his feet, tense with excitement, and began to run deeper into the woods, heading for the ruined greenhouse.

His head turned from side to side as he ran, looking for

another shimmering scrap of green that would lead him
to . . .

He didn't know what it was leading him to, but he knew
it was something he had to see.

Sewing Monsters

"MOM, look at this!"

Mozie rushed into the living room. The screen door banged behind him.

"Mozie, I asked you not to slam—"

"I know, Mom, but look!"

His mother was at her sewing machine and he held out his hand.

Already the scrap of green was losing its special luster.

"What am I supposed to be looking at—lettuce?"

"Mom!" he said, shocked.

She pulled her glasses down from her head. She used these glasses for detail work. She peered at the scrap of green through the round lenses.

"Mom, I think it's— Mom, I found this in the woods and . . . I mean, I know it doesn't look like much now, but when I found it, Mom, it was sort of, I don't know, luminous and . . . "

His words faded. Now she examined him through her thick lenses. "Mozic, is something wrong?"

"No, no. I just— Oh, never mind. Never mind!"

"Have you been back to that greenhouse?"

"No! Not all the way."

He turned quickly and left the room. He thought perhaps she would follow him into the kitchen and "hash it out" as she liked to say, but she did not. The drone of the sewing machine began almost at once.

His mother loved to sew and often lost herself in what she was doing, caught up in the shimmering fabric, the design, the dream. The only time she had been truly angry with Mozie was when she came home from shopping one October afternoon and found Batty at her sewing machine.

Batty and Mozie were going to be matching monsters for Halloween, and Batty wanted to run up some hoods for them. Mozie had said, "Mom wouldn't want us to use her machine." They were seven at the time, but Mozie was sure of what he was saying.

"She'll never know. Anyway, I sew all the time at home."

"Then let's go to your house."

"It's locked," Batty said quickly—too quickly it seemed to Mozie. He sat down. "I always have wanted to work one of these."

He turned on the light, and his face seemed to turn on at the same time. Mozie looked out the window to see if his mother was in sight.

"How do you get this up? How do you get this up?" Batty asked.

"I thought you said you could sew."

"I can, if I can get this up. All machines aren't alike, you know."

Mozie had the suspicion that this was Batty's first stint at any sewing machine, but he lifted the presser foot as he had seen his mother do. Then he went quickly back to the window to check for his mother.

Batty began to sew. He sewed in fits and starts, sometimes running off the cloth in his enthusiasm. Mozie peered critically over his shoulder at the tiny little jagged seam Batty was making.

"I love this," Batty said. He made his way around the first hood and stuffed it in his mouth, so his hands would be free for the second.

He was making a slightly less jagged seam around the second hood and was almost finished when he heard, "What is going on here?"

Batty and Mozie looked up to see Mrs. Mozer in the

doorway. Batty's mouth fell open in shock and his hood fell to his lap.

"We were sewing costumes," Mozie said. He was glad Batty was at the machine instead of himself, but he knew that wouldn't count for much with his mother.

"Do you realize that machine is the most valuable thing I own?"

"I'm sorry," Batty said. "I'm sorry." He got up so quickly he tipped over his chair.

"I was working in a bridal shop, altering brides' dresses on that machine, when the shop went out of business and I got the machine for back wages. That's how I got started at this." Her arms took in the pageant dresses hanging around the living room. Her look softened. "If you had asked me . . ."

Neither boy spoke.

"What were you making?" She picked up the hood that had fallen from Batty's mouth. "What are these?"

"They were hoods. We were going to wear them for Halloween," Batty managed to say.

"Oh, all right. I'll make the hoods for you." And she had turned out two hoods that looked as if they had come from a Disney movie. They wore them. They got a lot of compliments. But it had been the worst Halloween of Mozie's life.

Mozie continued to sit at the kitchen table, peering at the scrap of green before him. The sound of his mother's machine continued, and Mozie wondered if that was what he had heard, what had caused him to rush into the forest, to pick up a scrap of green and imagine it was the pod.

The phone rang. "Can you get that, Mozie?"

"Yes."

He picked up the phone. "Hello."

Valvoline said, "Mozie, I was so excited over my dress, I forgot to ask you about my necklace. Did you ever find it?"

"No, the greenhouse is ruined."

"Oh, I just hoped. I need that mustard seed. I'm wondering if you can buy them in the grocery store."

"I don't know."

"I really feel like I need something lucky. You know what happened to me on the way home?"

"No."

"This was so strange. I pulled into the old Esso station— where we parked that day—remember?"

"I remember."

"And the reason I stopped was because I heard this humming noise and I thought it was the car engine. But when I turned off the engine, the humming got even louder. And then, while I was sitting there, I saw the bushes behind the station moving."

Mozie glanced at the table where the scrap of green was drying, turning to dust.

"Moving?"

"Yes, like something was hiding in there. So I took off. I mean, I do not need to get mugged right before the pageant. But as I was driving away—this was the strange part."

She paused, and Mozie said, "Yes?"

"You aren't going to believe this, but it was like one of the bushes came to life. It just moved forward. Right out of the other bushes! I don't know what it could have been! You don't suppose somebody's after me, do you?"

Mozie remembered the day Valvoline had stepped beside McMummy. He remembered she had put her arms around the pod, rubbed her hand on the top, and made wishes. He remembered that was the first time he had ever heard the mummy purr.

"I don't think so," he said. "I hope not."

"Well, I tell you one thing, Mozie."

"What?"

"If I hear any more humming, I'm calling 911."

Pageant

"MY PHILOSOPHY of life is this . . ." Valvoline was saying.

She was on the stage of the Miss Tri-County Tech pageant in the dress Mrs. Mozer had created for her. Mozie and his mother were in the back row of the auditorium, watching.

Valvoline smiled into the microphone and then down at the row of judges in front.

". . . Be not what you are but what you are capable of being. Make every minute count. Spend time with yourself and your other loved ones. You only pass this way wunst."

"Once," Mrs. Mozer said beneath her breath.

As if the whisper had carried all the way to the stage, Valvoline said, "I mean 'once.' Thank you."

She got a lot of applause as she went back to join the line of other contestants. "Well, at least she's got on the prettiest dress," Mrs. Mozer said.

"That's true."

"And the little rose on the shoulder turned out to be just right."

"Yes," Mozie said.

There was a humming noise and Mozie shook his head to clear it. Ever since Valvoline had come onstage, he had been hearing this strange sort of purring sound. He wanted to rap himself on the side of the head to get rid of the sound.

Mozie had been slumped in his seat with his knees on the seat in front of him, but now he sat up straight. The humming noise was getting stronger now—so strong it might not be in his head.

The emcee was saying, "And now we move to the swimsuit portion of our pageant. While the contestants are changing into their swimsuits, the Tri-County Dancers will perform to 'Greensleeves.' "

Mrs. Mozer sat forward in her seat because she had made the costumes for the Tri-County Dancers.

The girls came onstage and a murmur of appreciation rose

from the audience. They wore long filmy green skirts that seemed to float in the air as the dancers leapt into place. A deeper green bodice was made up of leaves, with a large pink rose at the waist.

They held arches of roses in their hands, and as they swayed and bent to the music, the floral boughs caught the light and their green leaves shone like mirrors.

At the end of the number, after the applause, the dancers moved to the right of the stage. They held the boughs overhead, forming an archway for the contestants.

Mrs. Mozer leaned back. Mozie looked at her, but there was a frown on her face.

"Don't you like them?" he asked.

"It's not that. I just wish they'd fix the sound system. That humming is getting on my nerves."

"You hear it too?"

"Yes, and it's getting louder."

"The first contestant in the swimsuit portion is Miss Valvoline Edwards."

Valvoline came onstage in a white swimsuit. She walked carefully under the archway to the front of the stage.

There she turned. Mozie could see that Valvoline counted seconds the same way he had counted the time between the lightning and thunder on the night of the storm. He could see her lips moving in a silent one-thousand-and-one, one-thousand-and-two—

She never got to one-thousand-and-three because at that

moment there was a disturbance behind the Tri-County Dancers.

Screams were heard from the right of the stage. The screams increased until it seemed that everyone back there had taken up the habit.

The emcee looked worriedly at the righthand curtain. He tried to make a joke. "Hey, the excitement's supposed to be on the stage, folks, not off." The screaming continued. The emcee tried reason. "Come on, you guys, we're trying to have a pageant out here."

The curtain behind the dancers swayed. It sagged. It seemed something was clutching the curtain.

There was a ripping sound of tearing fabric, and the curtain dropped to the stage. There was a heavy thud, as if a large object had fallen with it.

"Just a minute, ladies and gentlemen," the emcee began because the audience was standing for a better look. "Keep your seats, please."

And then out of the folds of the fallen curtain rose something green. No one could see exactly what it was because the curtain shielded it like a cape, but Mozie knew. "McMummy."

The audience was on its feet now, blocking the stage from Mozie's view. "Get out of the way!" he cried. "What's happening, Mom? I've got to see this."

"It's—it's staggering forward," his mother said. "It's— Oh, get up on the seat."

She helped Mozie up, and over the heads of the crowd he saw McMummy struggling forward, reeling among the dancers, and the curtain that shielded him fell away. McMummy swirled to the center of the stage and stood for a moment, trembling in confusion.

The dancers drew back in alarm and threw their arches of roses as they turned and fled. The roses fell, some to the stage and some around McMummy's neck, giving him the appearance of having just won a horse race.

Now the people in front of Mozie were on their seats, again blocking the view. "What's happening?" Mozie cried.

"I can't see either," his mother said.

"This lady's fainted," a voice announced at the front of the auditorium. "Get back, everybody."

The crowd parted, and for a brief moment Mozie saw the green, luminous form. McMummy's arms flailed at the air as if to push back the lights, the excitement, the terror. Then McMummy turned and, throwing off the roses, made his way to the back of the stage. The screaming swimsuit contestants gave him room.

There was a stage door open at the rear and McMummy disappeared through it.

"I've got to help him," Mozie told his mother.

"What? Who?"

"McMummy."

"That thing from the pod? Stop! Where are you going?"

But Mozie was moving out of the auditorium and through the huge doors into the night.

"I'll be back," he said.

The Chase

MOZIE RAN through the parking lot at break-neck speed. He rounded the back of the Stuart Center and stopped.

He could hear screams of excitement from the open door, and people were beginning to spill out of the auditorium. Their voices asked the questions Mozie was asking himself. "Where did it go?" "Does anybody see it?"

Mozie headed for the dumpsters at the back fence. He had an intimation, like a silent echo, that McMummy had headed that way.

Behind the dumpster Mozie saw a patch of green caught on the fence. His heart thudded with dread.

He ran along the fence. There was more green.

He ran out of the center's parking lot, through a restaurant parking lot, and onto Main Street. The digital clock in the savings and loan said 8:32 P.M.

The town had installed new streetlights on Main, and Mozie had a clear view of the length of the street. Cinema III had just changed shows and people stood outside talking. Cars cruised idly, stopping at the stoplights, parking, pulling out of parking spaces.

Things were normal, so McMummy probably had not come this way.

He retraced his way through the restaurant parking lot, scrambled up a bank, and turned into the park. The park was poorly lit, and Mozie walked slowly down the path, watching on either side for another patch of iridescent green.

There it was—ahead, by the fountain. Mozie ran to the fountain. Green clung to the stone sides. In the moonlight, it could have been mistaken for moss.

Mozie ran his hand along it and moved to the light to examine it.

What was this stuff? Chlorophyll? And how much of it could a plant lose and still keep going?

He brushed his hands together and the green disintegrated and wafted to the ground like dust.

Mozie got the same feeling he had had earlier in the

evening—during the pageant—of time running out. It was such a strong sensation that in his mind he saw sand trickling through an hourglass, like in old movies when the director wanted to make sure even the dumbest viewer knew time was passing. The thought made Mozie break into a run.

He had only moonlight now to guide him, but the iridescent patches of green had become more plentiful.

As he ran, he felt as if he were being fast-forwarded through the scene. Everything was speeded up, even the beat of his pounding heart.

He paused to catch his breath. His side hurt. His throat was dry.

He wondered what he would do when he found McMummy. His only hope was that McMummy would recognize his voice. McMummy seemed to have an attachment for Valvoline. Of course, she had given him his first real human contact with her quick hug, her joyous "I didn't mean to hug it around the neck." Mozie had given only food and water, so the attachment could not be so strong.

The green turned off the path, and Mozie did too. He realized now that McMummy was heading back to the greenhouse. He would never make it. The greenhouse was miles away. Mozie didn't think he would make it either.

Mozie rounded a grove of trees and stopped. Ahead of him the green seemed to stretch out forever. It was plain what was happening.

Suddenly Mozie leaned against a tree. He put one arm around the trunk. He needed the tree for support.

He had just had the saddest thought of his life. He began to cry. Mozie never cried. Even when he wanted to—like that night in the guest room—he couldn't. He could not even remember the last time he had actually shed a tear.

Now it was as if the crying had been held in for nine or ten years, and like one of those trick cans of peanuts that fill the air with snakes when opened, the lid was off.

The sadness hit him so hard he sank to the ground, his back against the tree now, his face resting on his knees.

The thought that had done him in was that it had actually occurred to him to collect all these green scraps, to go back and start at the beginning and put them in a container.

And then he saw himself putting that container beside the box containing his father's things. And pretty soon he would be lining up another box and another and every important person in his life would be nothing but a box. He would never actually say farewell to anybody, just line them up in boxes.

It was the saddest thought in the world.

He wept until he could weep no more, and when the tears stopped at last, Mozie's breathing was ragged, his eyes were swollen, his nose was stopped up. He continued to sit where he was. Finally he dried his face on his shirt and got to his feet.

He walked very slowly down the stretch of green. He had cried so hard that when he came across the remains of McMummy, there were no tears left.

Stretched out on the floor of the forest, McMummy didn't look like anything special, just some debris left from the storm. Already the luminous quality was beginning to fade.

Mozie sighed. With one last look, he turned and started back the way he had come.

He retraced his steps, not looking down now, but ahead. He came through the park, scrambled down the bank, around the restaurant, and into the parking lot.

He walked through the doors of the Stuart Center. He crossed the lobby. He stood for a moment in the doorway of the auditorium.

He felt as if a decade, a lifetime, a century had passed, and yet, for the rest of the world, it had been no time at all.

The emcee was saying, "And now continuing with the talent portion of our pageant, here is contestant number ten.

"Each of us, at one time or another, has wanted to travel the earth like the Gypsies of old. And now Valvoline Edwards takes us on just such a trip with her baton-twirling rendition of 'Gypsy Rag.' "

Mozie slipped into the vacant seat beside his mother.

She patted his arm. "I'm glad you're back," she said.

Going Batty

 "SOMETIMES I THINK I'm living up to my name."

"How?" Mozie asked.

"Batty! I'm going batty!"

Mozie shifted the telephone. "What's happened now?" He settled down to listen.

"Did you see the morning paper?"

"No."

"Well, it's all about this big green thing that terrorized the Miss Tri-County Tech pageant. They're calling it the

Abominable Lettuce. And you know what I'm thinking? I'm thinking that could be McMummy. Maybe the pod wasn't empty after all."

Mozie straightened. "I haven't seen the paper. We don't take it. We—"

"And it's got a picture. It looks like what they did was take a file photo of Bigfoot and color it green. But—get this! One of the contestants' dad had his video recorder and got it all on tape! It's going to be on the seven o'clock news. Every hour a reporter comes on TV saying, 'Don't miss the Abominable Lettuce tonight at seven.'

"But if you look at this picture—the size is right. It's got sort of a little head and the body is roundish and—"

"I'll be right over," Mozie said.

He ran the four blocks to Batty's house and Batty was waiting with the newspaper.

"My dad thinks some college boys wrapped themselves up in kudzu for a prank. My sister thinks it was Fig Newton from her school, and I think it was McMummy. That's why I think I'm going batty."

"Then I'm going batty too," Mozie said.

"I think we ought to be out looking for him. I think we—"

Mozie cut off Batty's words with a wave of his hand. He took the paper and bent over the picture on the front page. CREATURE INTERRUPTS PAGEANT. There was a blurred shot of a green figure emerging from under a curtain with girls in swimsuits running in the background. Valvoline stood to one side with her hands on her hips.

"Hey, you were there, weren't you?" Batty said.

Mozie nodded. He began to read.

> Last night the Miss Tri-County Tech pageant was interrupted when a prankster wrapped in green leaves burst onto the stage during the swimsuit portion of the pageant.
>
> The pageant was resumed after the Abominable Lettuce, as it's being called, fled the scene. No one gave chase.
>
> Miss Valvoline Edwards, winner of the pageant, said, "I didn't think I would win when that whatever-it-was came onstage—some people will do anything to get attention— and then after it was all over and I was standing there in my swimsuit about to cry, I looked down and I could not believe it. There was my lucky mustard seed necklace—I lost it last week and now it turned up at my feet. I knew right then I was going to win."

Mozie let the paper drop to his lap. "Yes, I was there."

"So what happened?" Batty asked.

"What happened was that I knew something terrible was going to happen. I could feel it. All night there had been this humming noise and everybody thought it was in the loudspeaker and it kept getting louder and louder, and I knew exactly what it was."

Mozie paused to get his breath. Batty silently urged him on.

"It was McMummy. And I had just turned to my mom and was getting ready to say, 'I know what that noise is. Remember me telling you about the pod? That's what it is and we've got to do something.'

"But before I could speak, Batty, McMummy came onstage. It was awful. First he got tangled up in the curtain, and the whole curtain came down on top of him and the girls ran screaming around in their bathing suits. It was like somebody had seen a shark at the beach.

"And McMummy lumbered to his feet, and then he got tangled up in these arches the dancers dropped on his head, and for a minute he was in the lights, flailing at the noise, and I got a good look at him."

"So what was he like? This picture? He couldn't have looked like that." Batty slapped the newspaper in disgust.

Mozie shook his head. "I don't think I can describe him. You'll have to wait for the seven o'clock news."

"I can't wait. You have to tell me. Did he look like beans?"

"No."

"Lettuce?"

"Sort of. You know those trees in the old Walt Disney movies—like people would be lost in the forest and the trees would have faces and their branches would reach out like arms? Remember that?"

"Yes."

"Well, that was kind of what this was like. He was like half vegetable, half human, only there was no way you could say, 'The arms are human,' because they weren't. They were like—well, roots that had been pulled up out of the ground, with smaller roots for fingers.

"And you couldn't say, 'The face is human,' because the features were set back in wrinkles, and if he had a nose, I didn't see it.

"And you couldn't say, 'He moves like a human,' because there was something about his movement—well, he rolled sort of, and you couldn't say the sound was human because everybody but me thought it was something in the public-address system—"

"So what could you say was human?" Batty interrupted.

Mozie remembered Valvoline. He put his hand on his chest and patted the place just over his heart.

Batty looked at his friend. Several expressions crossed his face before he settled on mild disgust.

"But let's go look for it. You think it's around the Stuart Center? We could find it. We could go on *Sightings*. The park! I bet he would head for the park—"

"He did head for the park."

"You saw him? You followed him?"

"Yes. Anyway, he's gone now, so it doesn't matter."

"Gone? Like dead?"

Mozie nodded.

"You're going through all this human-vegetable assessment without telling me he's dead?"

"It's hard to tell."

"I tell hard stuff all the time!"

Mozie sighed as he began the long painful story of his search in the park—of finding one scrap of green after another and finally, after that long solid trail of green, finding the remains.

He left out only the part where he leaned against the tree and wept.

When he was finished, Batty was silent for a moment, and then he summed it up for himself, creating a new verb in the process.

"He saladed himself," he said.

Good-bye, Big Mac

MOZIE HAD NEVER HEARD the forest so full of sounds. Every bird that had survived the storm was singing with joy. The deep grass was alive with insect sounds. The air itself seemed full of energy.

Mozie felt he was the only unhappy thing in the forest. He made his way slowly through the trees to the clearing where the greenhouse had once stood.

It was seven-thirty in the evening. Mozie had watched the seven o'clock news with his mom. The report about

McMummy was one of the comedy news reports that the station was so fond of.

"The Northwest has its Bigfoot. The Himalayas have the Abominable Snowman. And now Downs City has the Abominable Lettuce. Here's Carol with the story."

The news report made it all seem like such a joke, like something out of a situation comedy—the huge green form—it did look sort of like a man-sized lettuce—careening onstage, doing what the reporter called "bringing down the curtain."

Valvoline in the foreground was so startled that she put her hands on her hips and stood bowlegged. The Tri-County Dancers forgot everything they knew about grace and lumbered around the stage like elephants.

And the reporter's final attempt at humor: "And as for the Abominable Lettuce, it was last seen being chased by a giant bottle of salad dressing."

The phone rang then. "That'll be for me," Mozie said.

Batty's voice said, "Can you believe that? Here is the story of the century—here is McMummy! And the stupid station is making jokes about a giant bottle of salad dressing."

"It was awful."

"We ought to go on television and tell them what really happened."

"They'd never believe us, Batty."

Mozie broke off his thoughts as he entered the clearing.

There was the smell of decay here now, and Mozie didn't want to stay, but he felt coming here was an important part of his good-bye.

He walked slowly, picking his way over the shards of glass. He thought he saw a scrap of green. He bent forward quickly, but it was only a leaf.

He was through here. There was nothing for him to do. Still, he could not bring himself to leave.

He remembered that Professor Orloff had said, "It's yours now." This was his, but all that was left was rotten plants and broken glass and rafters twisted like pretzels.

He continued to walk aimlessly around the ruins of the greenhouse. He heard a droning noise and he looked around quickly, bright with hope. Then he realized that the hum came from a plane heading for runway 28. He knew that he would probably be looking around with hope for the rest of his life whenever he heard a humming noise.

He was at the rear of the greenhouse now or what had once been the rear. He recalled that he had stood right here he put his feet on the spot—when he had first seen the pod.

He closed his eyes, and the memory washed over him like a wave. His heart beat faster, as it had then. His pulse quickened. He could smell the Nile again instead of the rotting vegetables.

He opened his eyes, smiling ruefully at himself. He glanced down. Half buried in the soft earth was something that . . .

He bent. As carefully as someone digging in an Egyptian ruin, someone uncovering a valuable artifact, he began to brush away the loose earth.

A green object—the green of new life. No, two of them, there were two!

Mozie picked them up and held them in his palm. They were beanlike, yet they did not have the shape of any bean he had ever seen.

He drew in his breath. They were in the shape of the pod. He held two tiny pods in his hands—miniature mummy cases—small rounded top, widening for the body.

Mozie got slowly to his feet. He continued to watch the two seed pods in his hand with awe.

Professor Orloff had given the greenhouse to him. These were his. These beans—human beans.

He closed his hand gently over the small objects. His mind raced with plans.

This afternoon he would come back with a shovel. He would scoop up the earth of the Nile and plant these pods in it.

He would search the area for the supply of Vitagrow. There might be some left. He would water these beans and take care of them until . . .

Mozie headed for the forest and broke into a run. As he ran home, the forest seemed to open a path for him like something out of a fairy tale.

There was his house—Crumb Castle #3.

"Mom, Mom, guess what!" he cried.

And Mozie ran into the house to show his mother the beans.

Betsy Byars has written more than thirty books for young people, including the Newbery Medal winner *The Summer of the Swans.* Six of her novels have been named ALA Notable Books, most recently *The Burning Questions of Bingo Brown,* which was also a *Booklist* Editor's Choice, "Best of the 80s." *The Burning Questions of Bingo Brown* was followed by *Bingo Brown and the Language of Love* and *Bingo Brown, Gypsy Lover,* all three of which were named *School Library Journal* Best Books of the Year. Ms. Byars has also received the American Book Award and the National Book Award, among many other awards and honors.

Betsy Byars lives in Clemson, South Carolina.